Loving Among
the Dead

Dahlia DeWinters

INDIGO HEART
PRESS

Loving Among the Dead

Copyright © 2014 by Dahlia DeWinters

ISBN

Editor: Kathleen Calhoun

Cover Artist: Indigo Heart Designs

Published in the United States of America

IndigoHeart Press
PO Box 750
Scotch Plains, NJ 07076

ACKNOWLEDGEMENTS

I am grateful to each and every person who assisted me in the writing of this book. Kassanna and Lynn Chantale helped me focus on pushing forward and were always there for commiseration, laughs, and the occasional kick in the pants. My sister listened to my crazy plots and did not laugh. My editor, Kat, provided sharp-eyed edits and creative insight that inspired me. Endless thanks to you all.

PROLOGUE

J udith Graham buried her parents on a Sunday. After a brief prayer, she placed her mother's favorite plant at the head of her grave, and her father's pipe—still full of tobacco ashes—at the head of his.

She brushed the dirt from her jeans, tucked the work gloves in her back pocket, and sat on the back deck sipping from a can of warm soda, watching the sun set. There were no tears. Her mother's pistol was at her side, the gunmetal gleaming in the fading orange light.

Would it have made a difference if she had gotten home sooner?

The letter, written on her mother's heavy monogrammed stationery, had been propped on the mantel, addressed to "Judith" in even, no-nonsense script. A marked contrast to the pale lavender paper, the black words indicated her father brought home the infection. She shot him in the back of his head when he started making gurgling, groaning sounds at the static on the television. Then she dug their graves, dragged him into his, and shot herself.

Stay hidden. Don't trust anyone. Her mother's final words to her. Jude was alone.

Her brother was south, somewhere, Alabama, the last she'd heard. Marcus did what he wanted, when he wanted. She was the good daughter who minded what her parents told her.

It wasn't so bad at first. Between the initial shock of her parents' deaths, and making defensive alterations to the house, there was no time or energy to think or feel much of anything.

Once the house was safe, the dehydrated food, water bottles, and toiletries arranged in the first floor den, the camp shower with its battery pump working and the lanterns loaded, there was lots of time to be lonely. Rereading favorite novels, patrolling the inside of the house, and searching for elusive ham broadcasts on the shortwave radio only filled up so much time.

She stopped looking at family photos because they made her cry, leaving her exhausted and listless, lying on the bed or the sofa or the floor for hours until the urge to pee roused her enough to move.

Her neighborhood was deserted. No walking dead bodies roamed the streets. Either her neighbors had gotten out or had been zombified in the confines of their homes, unable to juice up the physical memory necessary to open a door and escape. For that she was grateful. She'd had to smash too many zombie heads on her way back home from Philadelphia for her to revisit it with people she once knew.

Her one comfort was if things ever got out of hand, she had the gun. She hoped her aim would be good: blowing out the proper part of the brain to ensure she stayed dead wouldn't be easy. Though a gold member of her college rifle club, and a pretty good shot, she hadn't had the dubious opportunity of using herself as a target. And for that, there was only one chance.

The fourth week after she buried her parents, her mind wandered to thoughts of the gun. At least once each day, she would place it on the dining room table and stare at it, nudging it in slow circles with her index finger. Then she would pick it up and examine it from every angle, wondering how the barrel would feel in her mouth, under her chin, at the base of her ear. Would the recoil kick her hand upward and take the top of her head off, leaving her alive but paralyzed, unable to finish the job? Even as she ran her fingers around the trigger guard and down the hand grip, she wondered if she would have the nerve.

Her mother had been so practical and efficient. How must it have felt to have to kill her husband of thirty-plus years?

This time, Jude bit at her lip, fighting back the tears that always hovered, and pushed away from the table. It was better that she was alone—she would only have to make that decision for herself.

She established a routine, something to keep her sane in the long days stretching before her with no human communication. However, when her body demanded sleep, it was difficult to contain her thoughts. Sometimes when she dreamed, she imagined she could hear the wordless groans of the undead as they roamed, looking for fresh human meat to satisfy their never-ending hunger. She would jerk awake, drenched with sweat, a choked scream caught in her throat. Unable to return to sleep, she would rise and patrol the house with the battery lantern and her crowbar, straining to hear anything that would alert her to any presence in the house but her own.

Even after ensuring every lock was locked, plywood tight against the inside window frames, and doors barricaded, the relief of sleep would not overtake her. At these times she'd smoke a little weed, count the cracks in the ceiling, and cry some more, remembering her life before the monsters took over, obliterating everything that once brought her comfort. Eventually, the drug would take effect, and she would be able to fall into something resembling sleep.

CHAPTER ONE

The streets were empty, the air warm and quiet. Judith hummed a little as she walked, her crowbar thumping reassuringly against her thigh and her gun at her hip. The backpack that dangled off her arm was pink, the white visage of a cartoon cat staring out as she passed deserted houses and wrecked cars. The afternoon sun shone over her shoulder, warming her back as she strolled. She pushed open the door to the huge Stop and Shop.

The smell of rotted meat and decayed produce followed her all the way to the candy aisle. She took her time making her selections, considering the attributes of each selection before dropping the item in her bag. The area was deserted, had been for weeks. It was safe enough to venture out.

She was wrong.

The unwelcome shopping companion appeared wraith-like in front of her, a scary smile pasted on his face. Judith cursed herself for being so inattentive. She dropped her half-full backpack and pulled her gun out of its holster. *Show them the gun first, then they'll back off.*

This was not the case.

"Hi," he said, the tone a weak attempt at friendliness. Tall, sunburned and gaunt, he had dark eyes that held an intense brightness that scared her. His white t-shirt was smudged with dirt, as were his torn cargo pants. The leather vest was cracked and old. For a moment, Jude wondered why he was wearing a vest in the middle of summer.

The man took a step forward and the odor of old liquor and unwashed male swept over her. She took a step backward, her heart beating against her ribs.

The man's expression changed, became more cunning and sly.

"My name's Collie," he offered, as if they were meeting at a party. "What's yours?"

"Please don't make me shoot you." Judith took another step backward, her hand tightening on butt of her gun, her eyes on the man's sunburned face. Shoot the chest first, bigger target. Then shoot the back of the head.

So he doesn't get up again.

His eyes followed her hand and he shook his head, as if she were an errant child caught stealing candy.

"No need for that, pretty girl." He licked his cracked lips. "We can be friends, right?" He exhaled and another cloud of alcohol washed over her.

"No," she said, backing up another step. She didn't dare turn her back on him. "Leave me alone." Her lips trembled and she pressed them together. Where did he come from? How did he sneak up on her so quickly? "I just want to leave, okay?" She backed up again.

Sour body odor assaulted her nostrils seconds before a hand grabbed her from behind. The gun clattered on the floor and slid a few feet away. Jude sucked in a breath just as his other hand clamped around her throat. She didn't have a chance with the two of them.

"Got you, you whore." The second assailant's foul breath huffed past her nostrils. "You giving my buddy a hard time?" He squeezed her throat.

She struggled against his hold and he squeezed her throat, cutting off her air. Judith fought down the panic that rose in her belly. Was he going to choke her to death right here in the store?

"You stay still. Maybe I'll let you breathe every once in a while." The man who held her kept one hand around her throat while he fumbled over her body with the other, pinching and grabbing at her until she winced. "This is a hot one, here," he said, squeezing her breast with a huge, dirty hand. "Nice tits too. I'm warming her up for you, Collie." He kissed the side of her neck and laughed when she flinched away. "She'll put up a good fight. Sure you can handle her?" He released his hold on her throat and Judith sucked in a welcome breath, her mind screaming, but refusing to say the words they wanted to hear.

Please. No. Don't hurt me.

Because she knew for sure that they *would* hurt her, no matter how much she begged. In fact, begging would make it worse. Promising them she would do anything was moot. They would make her do any and everything.

All she wanted to was breathe. Her eyesight grew fuzzy around the edges as her oxygen was reduced. If she passed out, she would be good as dead, maybe even worse.

"Do you like that?" His whisper made her cringe. "I bet you do." The man's erection poked at her backside and his excited breath blew against her neck. He was having more fun choking her than he would have fucking her.

The clamping hand around her throat released, just a little, and she sucked in another welcome breath, fighting against her body's urge to struggle. With the two of them, that would only earn her a terrible beating.

Meanwhile, her original unwanted guest, Collie, watched, his eyes clouded with arousal as he watched his friend alternately fondle and choke her. Transported by the scene in front of him, he began to walk toward her, as if in a trance, his eyes focused on his partner's hand on her chest. "Yeah." He exhaled. "I can handle her."

Judith watched Collie approach, keeping her body limp and compliant. She needed every bit of oxygen and strength.

"You're not going to fight my friend, are you?" He stroked her neck, the delicate touch incongruous with the cruelly smothering clamp of a moment ago.

Judith nodded her head, concentrated on breathing and the man in front of her. She still had her crowbar.

"I won't fight." Her voice came out shaky and teary, defeated.

The dirty creep grinned at her, a smile like a picket fence with a couple of slats missing. "Sure you won't." He came even closer, rubbing his crotch through the stained pants. "We're going to have a good time you and me. Maybe you could be my girlfriend."

Be his girlfriend? Now that was a fate worse than death. Judith waited until he was close enough and she kicked up and out as hard as she could, the steel toe of her boot slamming into his crotch so deep that she swore she touched bone. Or at least a boner. *Heh.*

Collie let out an ear-splitting howl. Jude didn't wait for him to hit the floor before she snatched her crowbar out of its Velcro loop and swung it up and across her body, catching her breath-play buddy on the side of his head, the tempered steel hitting his skull with a choppy *thunk*. His hand dropped from her throat. Pulling downward, she hoped to scrape his ear off the side of his head.

"Fuck!" he screamed and fell to his knees.

A quick glance behind her found him holding bloody fingers to the side of his head, a scrap of flesh on the floor.

Judith looked around for her gun and not seeing it, hopped over the prone body of Collie, who was now lying in a brownish pool of his own alcohol-laden vomit. She spit on him, then dashed through the aisles to the exit, planning a quick getaway before either of them recovered.

In the parking lot, there was the rest of the crew, lounging against a van that had its doors open.

Judith froze for only a second, then began to run.
****

Judith raced across the macadam parking lot in the late summer afternoon.

The section of her consciousness that wasn't urging her boots to go faster registered that the men were getting closer. Her Doc Martens, which she had been eyeing in the store window since before The Event, were black with red roses, thudded on the ground as she ran.

A simple visit to the long since abandoned supermarket had turned into a run for her very life, one of many runs for her life that had taken place in the past two months.

The two months since the dead began to walk again.

The men's footfalls on the pavement were loud and fast and getting closer. They wanted her. Badly. She was a gazelle, albeit a slow, awkward one, running from a pack of hungry, relentless lions.

They would not, could not catch her. She'd rather be ripped apart by zombies than be at the mercy of these ferocious men, who took advantage of the lack of law and order to explore their basest instincts and desires. The preview she'd gotten in the supermarket had been enough. They would keep her around for their physical needs until she was too ragged to use anymore, then they would kill her. It would not be an easy death.

They wouldn't catch her.

The buzzing of the cicadas in the trees accompanied the thud of her feet and the labored rasping of her breath in and out of her aching lungs. The boots were heavy and hot, jarring her legs all the way up to her hips each time her feet hit the ground. She grit her teeth against the discomfort and kept up her pace, resisting the urge to look over her shoulder to see how close they were.

Don't look back, something might be gaining on you.

One of the men had almost caught her as she dashed out of the store; her skin held the memory of his sweaty hand slipping down her arm as she twisted away and ran.

Behind her, the engine of the van chugged into life. They were going to corner her in the parking lot, but if she could make it to the alley, she would have a better chance. The van couldn't fit down the alley.

Sweat ran in a trickle between her breasts. The back of the t-shirt was already slickly wet with her efforts. She ran a tongue over her dry lips and urged her feet to go even faster.

"Stop! We're not going to hurt you! Stop!" a rough male voice yelled.

Judith would have laughed if she could have spared the breath. *Not going to hurt you.....much.* The division between the two buildings offered dark salvation. She darted down the narrow, trash-littered alleyway. The end of the passage offered freedom.

Until shadowy figures appeared in front of her.

Making an abrupt U-turn, she attempted to go back the way she came, but the van was blocking the other end of the alley.

She turned again, her mind racing in a thousand directions. The men walked toward her at a leisurely pace, sure that she was trapped.

"We've got you now. Nowhere to go," one of them called, closing the distance between them.

"You'll be sorry you ran!" shouted another, and cruel laughter echoed toward her.

Judith looked upward then scanned the alley. There must be some way of escape.

The service entrance door to the drugstore. She reached with one trembling hand and pulled, yanked at the edge of the rusted metal.

It was closed, the metal lip almost flush against the jamb.

There was no doorknob on the outside of the door. Nothing to pull or tug at.

Judith let out a small cry and kicked at the door in frustration, her boot leaving a black mark on the dull surface. *Where to go?* Her mind raced through the possibilities as the peephole stared back at her in the waning light, mocking her and her need to hide and to hide now.

The catcalls and taunts grew closer on both sides. They knew she was trapped and were dragging out their success of capturing her. There had been only two in the store, but she had no idea how many had been in the group that had waited outside. Where was she going to go now?

Judith kicked the door again. *Dammit.* Her stomach roiled and she had to fight to keep from vomiting from fear. Her eyes darted from one side to another, watching the predators approach. They were going to tear her apart.

Behind her, the door let out a loud, rusty screech as it opened and Judith was jerked backwards into the darkness.

CHAPTER TWO

Judith Graham buried her parents on a Sunday. After a brief prayer, she placed her mother's favorite plant at the head of her grave and her father's pipe, still full of tobacco ashes, at the head of his.

She brushed the dirt from her jeans, tucked the work gloves in her back pocket and sat on the back deck sipping from a can of warm soda, watching the sun set. Her mother's Ruger LCR .357 was at her side, the gunmetal gleaming in the fading orange light. There were no tears.

Would it have made a difference if she had gotten home sooner?

Her mother's note indicated that her father brought home the infection. She shot him in the back of his head when he started making gurgling, groaning sounds at the static on the television. Then, she dug their graves, dragged him into the yard and shot herself.

Judith was alone. Her brother was down south, somewhere, Alabama, the last she heard. Marcus did what he wanted, when he wanted. She was the good daughter, who minded what her parents told her.

Neither of them were here now to tell her what to do next.

It wasn't so bad at first. Between the initial shock of her parents' deaths and the necessary alterations to the house to defend it from the zombies and the human predators, there was neither time nor energy to think or feel much.

Once the house was safe, the dehydrated food, water bottles and toiletries arranged in the first floor den, the camp shower with its battery pump working and the battery lanterns loaded, there was lots of time to be lonely. Reading by lantern light, patrolling the inside of the house and searching for elusive ham broadcasts on the shortwave radio only filled up so much time.

She stopped looking at family photos because they made her cry, leaving her exhausted and listless, lying on the bed or the sofa or the floor for hours until the urge to pee roused her enough to move.

Her neighborhood was deserted. No walking dead bodies roamed the streets. Either her neighbors had gotten out or had been zombified in the confines of their homes, unable to juice up the physical memory necessary to open a door and escape. For that she was grateful. She had to smash too many zombie heads on her way back home from Philadelphia for her to revisit it with people she once knew.

The one comfort was that if things ever got out of hand, she had the Ruger. She just hoped her aim would be good: blowing out the proper part of the brain to ensure she stayed dead wouldn't be easy. Though a Gold member of her college rifle club and a pretty good shot at that, she hadn't had the dubious opportunity of using herself as a target. And for that, you only got one chance.

The fourth week after she buried her parents, her mind wandered to thoughts of the Ruger. At least once each day, she would place it on the dining room table and stare at it, nudging it in slow circles with her index finger. Then she would pick it up and examine it from every angle possible, wondering how the barrel would feel in her mouth, under her chin, at the base of her ear. Would the recoil kick her hand upward and take the top of her head off, leaving her alive but paralyzed, unable to finish the job? Even as she ran her fingers around the trigger guard and down the hand grip, she wondered if she would even have the nerve.

Her mother had been so practical and efficient. How must it have felt to have to kill your husband of thirty-plus years?

This time, Judith bit at her lip, fighting back the tears always hovered and pushed herself away from the table. It was better that she was alone – she would only have to make that decision for herself.

She established a routine, something to keep her sane in the long days that stretched before her with no human communication, but when her body demanded sleep, it was difficult to contain her thoughts. Sometimes when she dreamed, she imagined that she could hear the wordless moans and groans of the undead as they roamed, looking for fresh human meat to satisfy their never-ending hunger. She would jerk awake, drenched with sweat, a choked scream caught in her throat. Unable to return to even fitful slumber, she would rise and patrol the house with the battery lantern and her crowbar, ears straining to hear a noise that would alert her to any presence in the house but her own.

Even after ensuring every lock was locked, plywood tight against the inside window frames and the doors barricaded, the relief of sleep would not overtake her. At these times she'd smoke a little weed, count the cracks in the ceiling and cry some more, remembering her life before the monsters took over, obliterating everything that once brought her comfort. Eventually, the weed would take effect and she would be able to fall into something resembling sleep.

* * * *

The stockroom door scraped shut mere seconds before her newfound enemies began banging on the door. Whoever had pulled her in here, and that whoever was decidedly male, judging from the hard body pressed against hers in the dark. Judith struggled and kicked against the strong body holding her, further terror rising in her chest, eyes seeing nothing in the complete darkness. It was one of them, one of them who had cut through the store to trap her. Now he was going to deliver her to his friends. Fear and revulsion fueled her panic.

"Be still, girl." The voice was male, soft and whispery. "We might not be alone." His lips brushed her ear, made her shiver.

Those few words gave her assurance that he was not one of the men who had chased her. Judith closed her eyes against the darkness and summoned stillness, her heart thrumming like a live wire. He was right. Ghouls, shufflers, zombies whatever you wanted to call the undead, staggering hunks of what used to be human might be lurking in here with them. She relaxed, expecting her rescuer to release his grip across her breasts, but at that moment, a loud banging on the door made them both jump.

"Open this door, bitch! We know you're in there."

"Shit," he whispered.

There was movement in the darkness. It was a stealthy, dragging sound, like something moving in the dark when it thought that no one else could hear. Something ready to sidle up behind you in the dark and blow its fetid breath down the back of your neck just before ripping a mouthful of flesh from your throat.

Judith's stomach turned to ice and she trembled in the stranger's arms. She had seen and killed enough of those things to last her a lifetime. The thought of them being right there in the dark with her? A small, terrified sound squeaked out of her throat.

The man clamped a hand over her mouth.

"Shhh," he breathed in her ear and she shivered again.

The nasty, sliding sounds increased, excited by the hammering at the door.

Oh dear God there was more than one.. Judith barely kept herself from moaning aloud.

Adding to the sounds from the stockroom door, faint rustling and voices carried to her. They were still looking for her, filling the main area of the drugstore with their shouts while the other waited in the alley. Neither group was aware that something else was more than willing to make them the catch of the day.

The stranger dropped his hand from her mouth. "Stay with me, okay? This next part's gonna be a little rough."

She nodded, somehow comforted by his arm still around her waist. The group from the store burst into their area, their flashlights and loud voices stirring up the predators in the dark.

Fresh panic surged through her. She was going to be eaten alive, in the dark. All because of her damned sweet tooth.

"Come with me." The man pulled her backwards again. The sound was muffled and rough cloth brushed her face. The scent of cinnamon gum on his breath warmed her. Walls closed in around her and cloth brushed against her face. She realized that he had pulled her into a closet. A small one.

"We'll wait it out in here," he said. "I hope they enjoy their party."

CHAPTER THREE

Should have gone south when I had the chance. Sky Beckett told himself. Internet radio broadcasts, when they came through, said that things were better in the South. More room to spread out, more places to hide. Most of New Jersey was crowded, too metropolitan. People were piled on top of one another in apartment buildings and high rises. Even in the suburbs, some of the homes were built so closely together that you could cuss a cat and get fur in your mouth, as his mother would say. No wonder the infection moved so quickly.

Summer made traveling much easier. He couldn't imagine trying to make this trek in the deep freeze of a northern winter. Stay out of sight, travel only during the day. For some reason the monsters didn't like the daytime and the summer made them lethargic. They also rotted faster, rendering them less harmful. The south was a perfect place. And it was home. A perfect mix of urban, suburban and downright gun-totin' rural.

He'd traveled to New Jersey with the noble intention of teaching. It was the hippy gene he inherited from his mother. Despite his laid-back demeanor, he gained the respect of his students by being tough but fair, and earned the respect of his older, more experienced colleagues by his classes' passing scores on the state tests.

Granted, he had been laid off and rehired four times in his five year career because the school board played fast and loose with taxpayers' funds. Non-tenured teachers were always the first to go, and since he was always fired and rehired every year, it was always technically his first year. It was fine by him because he was able to collect unemployment during the summer and walk right back into his old classroom in September, guaranteed. Who else were they going to find to teach science in an inner-city high school?

His summer had been uneventful. Unemployment money deposited on time, there was money for liquor and pot and the library offered an air-conditioned place to read and relax. Fine and dandy, that is, until one of his roommates, Troy, brought the infection home the second week of summer vacation. Bleary-eyed from his afternoon nap, Sky had at first thought that Troy was high, a not unusual state for either of them during summer break. Just in time, however, the grunting and the milky eyes told him Troy was more than tripped out on good weed. And the smell. As many zombie movies as he'd seen, they didn't prepare him for the smell of three -day old garbage that what-used-to-be-Troy brought with him.

He'd bashed in his roommate's skull with his aluminum baseball bat and puked his lunch on top of Troy's still twitching body. It took him a half hour before he could gather himself enough to heave his now-dead-for-real friend out of his bedroom window into the alley below.

His other roommate, Robert, never came back. Telephone calls to friends and his family didn't go through. Beyond what he heard or saw in the media, he didn't know what was going on.

So he stayed put until the groans and sounds of the restless undead in the streets grew too much for him. Once the food ran out and the radio broadcasts stopped, Sky figured he'd better make tracks south.

Weeks later, after walking through an abandoned residential neighborhood that was surprisingly zombie free, he spotted the familiar red and white sign of a drugstore. His backpack, well-worn from weekend hiking trips, was nearly full of supplies, but he needed antibacterial ointment and was hoping to snag some soda. It would be warm, yeah, but the caffeine and sugar would be a welcome refresher.

Once inside, he noticed that the shelves seemed relatively untouched, save for a few items on the floor here and there. He paused first before he moved any farther, listening for any indication of movement. Spotting a bottle of glass cleaner on the floor, he scooped it up and tossed it across the store. After the initial crash, there was silence. If there was anyone in the store, especially the undead, they would be moving around.

Sky breathed through his mouth as he counted off a full minute on his self-winding watch. His gum, which he chewed as a defense against unpleasant fragrances was no match for the scent of rotten broccoli and dead bodies in such an enclosed space. At least there were no answering sounds, no furtive dragging that indicated anyone, living or undead, was here with him. He snatched a couple packs of gum from the candy display beneath the cashier counter, opened a pack and popped yet another stick in his mouth, savoring the burn of the cinnamon flavoring on his tongue as he allowed the aluminum wrapper to flutter to the floor. He shoved the packs in his pocket and took a quick look around. The soda cases were usually up front. He could grab a few bottles and then scout a place for the night.

Late afternoon sunlight streamed through the high windows providing him with more than enough illumination. His shoes made no sound on the carpet floor and his breathing was loud in his ears. Sky picked through the aisles, grabbing cough syrup and anything else he thought he might need, working his way toward the goldmine of sodas at the front of the store. He hummed under his breath, enjoying the respite from the sun and the heat outside.

Behind him, the sound of doors slamming and loud excited voices made him freeze, holding a small box of antibacterial ointment in his hand. *Who the hell are these people?*

Too many teacher workshops on mob mentality, bullying and gangs had made him leery of organized groups on his trek south. Group dynamics could shift so quickly that he would find himself in the middle of some bullshit if someone in the group took a dislike to him. Oddly enough, to pick on the individual while you were in a gang was somehow a show of strength.

Today, he wasn't going to be that individual.

Sky hurried to the street side of the store, where the stockroom was located. In his other life, BZ, Before Zombies, he'd been a CVS devotee and had endeared himself to the staff to the point where they knew him by name and he knew the store like the back of his hand. Most CVS stores were laid out the same way and this one did not disappoint.

He pushed open the stockroom door, pulled his flashlight and his bat, foregoing the gun stuck at the small of his back. A gun made too much noise. It might be zombie central in there and he wasn't taking any chances. With a few careful swings of the flashlight, he determined the immediate area was clear. Pushing his way through a pair of swinging doors, he found himself in a room with smaller tables and a vending machine in the corner. The employee break room.

Sweeping the flashlight around, the beam picked up half-eaten, putrefied lunches on a table and an unopened bottle of soda. Unable to resist, he twisted off the top and took a long drink of the warm, sugary liquid.

Another swing of the flashlight showed him the stockroom door and he wound his way through the tables towards freedom. Just as he reached the door, there was a thump from the outside. He put his eye to the peephole.

The woman standing outside whipped her head to the right, as if looking for something. There was another kick and a scrabbling sound as she tried to open the door.

Without thinking, Sky shoved the door open and pulled her inside.

* * * *

Because the closet was so small, she remained crammed against him. He could feel her ribcage expanding and contracting with each breath and her bottom pressing into his lap. Sky closed his eyes, praying for control. It had been too long since he had even touched a woman, much less had a firm tush shoved against him in such an intimate manner. For now he hugged the good smelling woman to him and enjoyed the weight of her body against his. If this is what he had to endure to keep her (and him) safe, it might be an awful, terrible burden but someone had to take the job.

Her heart beat like a jackrabbit's against his chest. She had no pack, no gear. She must be staying nearby. He inhaled her scent again, an intoxicating mix of vanilla and something floral.

Sky could see the beams of her pursuers' flashlights through the crack at the bottom of the door.

"She's gotta be in here. No way she could have gotten out the front without getting nabbed," one of them snarled as they pushed the back door open with a screech. The men from the alley joined the conversation.

"That cunt fucked up my balls, man, I can feel 'em swelling up. And she almost took off Andy's ear."

"Fuck yeah. When we find her, first thing I'm gonna do is—What the fuck! Collie, look out!"

The woman pressed back against him, crushing him into the back wall. The gun dug into the small of his back, grinding against his vertebrae. He slid his arm under her breasts and pulled her still tighter against him, letting her draw comfort from the proximity of their bodies. She trembled so much that he swore he could hear her teeth chattering even over the shouts and confusion from the other room.

Sky put his mouth close to her ear. "We'll wait till they're busy with your friends, then we'll go."

The screams and the cries continued as well as the wet, ripping sounds of human flesh being consumed. The groans of the zombies grew louder and more frantic as the attack continued; the flashlight beams jerking around as their owners were either attacked, torn apart or ran for their lives. Bodies smacked wetly on the concrete floor as the screams of the living dissolved into pitiful moans and their cries for help went unanswered.

The woman shivered and shook against him, no matter how tightly he held her. There was wetness on his bare arm and he realized that she was crying. "Don't cry for them, honey," he whispered in her ear. He smoothed her hair back away from her sweaty face. "They woulda done worse to you, I can guarantee you that."

After the cacophony of screams and shouts, an eerie silence reigned, punctuated by the occasional groan and tearing, squishy noises. His watch ticked off the seconds.

"Come on." He stood the best he could in the cramped space, pulled her up with him. "We can go."

"No, no," she pleaded, a death grip on his arm. "I can't go out there. I won't. We'll wait until they leave."

"They can't leave," he whispered. "We need to go now, while they're distracted with their eating."

He grabbed her around the waist and yanked her against him. Sky rarely manhandled a woman, but he couldn't leave her here and she wasn't going to stop him from leaving.

"But--"

"Be quiet and come with me. It'll be fine." He wasn't as sure as he sounded, but something in his voice must have convinced her because she relaxed against him.

With his gun at the ready, he nudged the closet door open with the toe of his boot.

Chapter Four

The yellow beam of the flashlight picked up every crimson streak and splash on the floor and walls. Puddles of thick gore and unidentifiable piles of wet matter were the only sign of the gang that had chased them. *Abattoir.* Sky eased the woman among the feasting zombies. He breathed through his mouth, filtering the air through the wad of gum tucked in one cheek. Blood didn't bother him, but why smell it if you didn't have to?

Keeping the light pointed in front of him, his ears listening for the slightest change in the feeding sounds, he negotiated their way to the outer door. The woman made no sound, but held his left arm in a grip so painful, it would leave bruises. But at least she wasn't making any noise. For now, the zombies were so engrossed in gorging themselves on fresh kill that they could slip out unnoticed. *For now.* Moving quickly and quietly was the key. He didn't take an easy breath until both of them were in the alley and the door was closed behind them.

"Are you all right?" He did a quick visual check for cuts and bruises, noting the way her t-shirt pulled across her breasts. He forced his gaze back up to her face.

The woman wiped her eyes with shaking, dirty hands, leaving a smudge across her cinnamon-colored nose. Her hair was pulled into a haphazard ponytail on the top of her head, and her brown eyes were tired in the late afternoon light. Behind the dirt, she was a fine-looking woman. And, despite himself, he wanted to have a peek at that behind that he had felt but not seen in the darkness.

"Thank you, I'm fine, " she said in a creaky voice, turned and walked away. "I appreciate your help. Good luck."

A few strides and he caught up with her. "Where are you staying?" he asked.

"I have a place." She didn't pause to look at him. "Leave me alone. I thanked you, didn't I?"

"You have a place around here?"

"Yes, I do." This time she stopped. "There are plenty of houses around here. You can find your own place."

Sky glanced around at the unfamiliar neighborhood. If he hadn't been distracted with saving her ass, he would have had time to scout and find his own place. You would think she had the heart to offer him at least one night's stay, but he understood. Given the way some people acted after the outbreak, having a heart could get you murdered outright.

"Look," he put a hand on her arm to prevent her from walking away again. "I just need a place to stay for one night."

She stepped away enough that his hand dropped off her arm and gave him the once over.

"And why should I even trust you?"

"I could have left you back there in the alley with those thugs." He winced as he prepared to say the next part, but he needed a place. "Or with the zombies."

The woman bit at her bottom lip as she considered. "Your point is taken." She nodded. "One night. You be gone in the morning." She began walking. "Get moving. It's getting dark."

Sky followed her, his long strides matching her fast pace. The sky was losing light and he imagined he heard murmurs and groans from shadowed alleys. He didn't like being out this time of night; it's when *they* became more active and you couldn't see.

"Are we almost there?" It was like he was carrying five cinderblocks on his back. His shoulders screamed for a rest. They had progressed into a residential neighborhood and he didn't trust the bushes and decorative fences that could be hiding anything.

"Couple more blocks." Their feet scraped against the sidewalk. "What's your name? I'm Judith."

"I'm Sky."

"Sky?" She laughed, a soft ladylike like sound that drifted away into the oppressive silence. "Nice to meet you, Sky. I guess I don't need to shake your hand. I practically gave you a lap dance in the closet."

Judith explained that not many zombies wandered past her house and that she suspected she was the only one staying in the immediate neighborhood. She wasted no words when she spoke, leading him past crashed cars and houses with wide-open doors. The light was fading even more rapidly, hurrying their pace.

* * * *

"We're here."

Sky played his flashlight over the house. Judith's place was a tall Colonial. The first floor windows had been nailed over with plywood. The front yard, an expanse of unmowed grass about a foot high, was partially boarded by a tall iron fence on either side, but because the house was set back from the street and on a slight rise, it was less vulnerable than he first thought.

They walked down the driveway towards the garage where there was a six foot gate. Behind the iron gate, which Judith opened with a key she wore around her neck, the backyard was completely enclosed with a decorative concrete wall.

"Take off your pack," she said, walking along an overgrown brick path. "We'll bring it in through the basement. You won't be able to get through the window with that on your back. Plus, we have to climb."

The fire escape ladder she indicated with wave of her hand looked sturdy enough but made him swallow past a sudden lump in his throat. It couldn't have been more than twelve or so feet off the ground but it might as well been fifty. She couldn't just go inside then open the back door for him? On the other hand, did he want to wait outside in the fading light for her to let him in? Sure, there was the concrete wall, but anything could be roving out there in the dark.

Sky dropped his pack as she requested and Judith preceded him up the fire escape ladder. He followed, his heart pounding in his ears and his mouth dry. Though the ladder had only twelve rungs, (he counted) it seemed like an eternity before he was inside. He collapsed on the rug, sucking in deep breaths to fight off the nausea that rose in him. Funny that he didn't feel sick while he was climbing. It was only after he made the mistake of looking down just before he climbed through the window that he realized how high up he was.

Judith rolled up the ladder and partially closed the window."Are you okay?" She crouched down to where he sat on the carpet floor.

"Fine." He stood up on shaky legs.

She stood with him, scrutinizing him in the glow of the lantern. "You're afraid of heights."

"A little," he admitted.

Judith smiled, patted his arm. "The doors are barricaded from the inside and since I was alone, it was more prudent to use the ladder. But now that there are two of us, we can use the door."

Now he was really embarrassed. "There's no need to..."

She waved away his protests. "There's enough to be afraid of. Let's eliminate what we can. Take a load off." She indicated the room they were now in and its chairs, low coffee table and sofa. "I'm going to wash my hands."

* * * *

The smile stayed on Judith's as she walked down the dim hallway. She'd honestly thought Sky was going to pass out. Truth be told, the ladder freaked her out too.

In the bathroom, she turned on another lantern she'd set up on the back of the now useless toilet and dipped her hands in a bucket of fresh water she'd set on the closed toilet lid.

She washed her hands and swiped at the smudge on her face, attempted to smooth her curls into submission. Barring that, she pulled a few crinkly strands forward, then stopped, meeting her own eyes in the mirror.

Slowly, she lowered her hands from where they had been fussing with her hair. She wasn't like this, had never been a woman who cared what a man thought about her. She'd had her books, her studies and her parents. Now she had none of that and didn't want to lose anything else. Intimacy was the enemy, made you want and need and desire, and the way things were going, made you mourn.

She left the bathroom and crossed to her bedroom, removed her boots. This was the time to behave like a survivor. This wasn't a *date*. She padded down the hallway in her sock-feet to rejoin her guest.

Sky had pulled himself together and was sitting, eyes closed, in one of the wingback chairs. Her parents had established this room as sort of a sitting room for the second floor, a place to sneak away if either of them couldn't sleep in the middle of the night. A few weak beams of the full moon filtered through the half-open curtains, casting glowing slivers on the rug.

Was he sleeping? She stood in the doorway and allowed her gaze to follow the long lines of his body, from his almost brand new looking hiking boots to the jeans to the inked vine-like lines twisting up his forearms to his mid-biceps. She already knew the biceps were more than substantial; she had tried her best to squeeze the blood out of them as they picked their way through the horde of feasting zombies.

Shivering at the memory, she must have made a small noise because he opened his eyes . Her heart gave a little leap in her chest.

Caught staring.

"Is your given name Sky?" To cover her embarrassment, she crossed to the stack of bottled water in the corner, pulled out a bottle and offered it to him. It was the least she could do.

"Yeah. My mother was...is a modern hippie." He took the bottle of water and twisted off the cap. "I sure do appreciate you offering me a place here."

Some color had returned to his face; even in the light of the lantern he had looked pale and sickly after his climb. The short brown beard that covered the lower half of his face accentuated the youthfulness of his eyes, as if he were a teenager trying to prove his manliness by growing facial hair. *With that body he didn't have to prove a thing.* Mentally, she rolled her eyes at her own thoughts. *You're being ridiculous.*

"How old are you, Sky?" She sat on the floor behind the table, opposite him.

"Thirty."

"Me too," she offered. "Well, I'll be thirty in August." She searched for something else to say. Small talk had never been one of her strengths and after being alone for so long, she was awkward and self-conscious. "Where are you from?"

"Tennessee, but been in New Jersey more than a couple years. I teach..well, used to teach, science in Newark."

"A science teacher?" Again, her eyes found the scrolled lines that wrapped around his forearms.. "They hired you with those tattoos? It looks like you have the Dead Sea Scrolls on your arms."

"Yeah." He extended and arm, examined the markings. "I had to wear armbands to cover them when I wore a short-sleeved shirt."

Judith sat back and took a thoughtful sip from her bottle. "Teachers are a lot cooler than they were when I went to school." *Better looking too.* This time, she smirked at her own thoughts.

"What's funny?"

Unable to wipe the smile from her face, she shook her head once, then changed the subject. "You can stay here. I've got supplies and there's water for washing up." She plopped her water bottle down as she got up. "Let's go get your pack."

CHAPTER FIVE

From what he could see by the lantern Judith carried and his own flashlight, she had quite the setup. The living room boasted a huge fireplace and high, beamed ceilings. The rugs were soft underfoot, lining the hardwood floors that gleamed even in the dim light.

The basement was one large room, divided by the stairwell, its walls lined with metal shelves groaning with supplies. He counted at least ten cases of water stored in one corner and brown cardboard boxes labeled with various foodstuffs stacked against another. When Judith said she had plenty of supplies, she wasn't kidding. There were supplies there enough to sustain a family of four for at least a year including washing powder, batteries and what looked like a floor to ceiling pile of army blankets.

"This is all yours?" He swung the beam of his flashlight around, noting the shuttered basement windows. "I mean you got all these supplies?"

"Not exactly." She didn't elaborate and he didn't press. Let her keep her secrets.

He helped her move a couple of boxes of dehydrated food to the side so that Judith, standing on a pile of two books, could open the basement window.

"Get your pack."

He did just that and watched as she watched the small, rectangular window, then secured the shutters. Sky hefted his pack on his back and followed her back up the basement stairs, his mind full of questions, but his eyes on that generous behind of hers.

Back in the sitting room, Judith managed to create a pretty good tasting meal from the dehydrated food, canned fruit and a little camp stove she set up to vent next to a window.

Dinner was a quiet meal. They both had been alone for so long that it was almost impossible to have a conversation with another human being. Even the questions that he'd had for Judith faded away as he ate, his taste buds waking to the flavors in the lasagna with meat sauce.

"Meat is a relative term, I think," she commented as she picked at her share of the meal.

Dessert was warmed peaches with cinnamon crumble.

Sky thought it was the best meal he'd had in weeks.

After cleanup, which consisted of dropping paper plates and forks in a garbage bag, she brought out a little radio and cranked the handle, revving it up. She then began scanning the stations, turning the knob a millimeter at a time.

"Most of the radio went out weeks ago," he said.

"This is shortwave, not regular radio," she glanced up at him, her eyes luminous in the battery lantern's glowing light. "It picks up ham radio broadcasts."

"Like somebody broadcasting from their basement?"

"Yeah. Or a bunker." She stopped talking as she turned the dial, her eyes focused on a point in the far distance, listening.

Her hair was no longer in the ponytail, instead it fell in tight, curly sprigs around her face. The lantern cast highlights on her hair, lightening the brown to almost blonde. He watched as she chewed on her full bottom lip, grasping it between her teeth and letting it slide almost out before biting down on it again. It was the sexiest thing he had ever seen a woman do.

Whatever she was listening for didn't come through because she turned the radio off and replaced it on the shelf. Resuming her seat across the low table from him, she smiled brightly. "Nothing tonight. Maybe tomorrow."

"What are you listening for?"

Judith shrugged. "I don't know. An official broadcast? Proof that there are regular folks still living, hiding out away from zombies and creepy mob rapists? Maybe a place where we can all go?" She trailed off, her fingers tracing patterns on the table's smooth wood surface. "Doubtful, though."

"There's always hope."

Judith heaved a huge sigh. "Maybe I should be more realistic. You've been out there, right? Am I just crazy?"

"I don't know, Judith, I really don't." He was unsure of what answer she wanted, so he gave her the honest one. "But I do know that I haven't seen any camps."

Her next words came out in a rush. "I'm not sure how much longer I can live like this, but I won't leave. It's safe here. Believe me I know. I traveled here by myself, from Philadelphia." She drummed her fingers as she spoke in a hushed, intense whisper. "Most of the way I made it by car, but I ran out of gas and had to walk the last ten or so miles. I had to kill those things with a crowbar. I didn't have a gun." She grimaced and grabbed a napkin, began tearing it into small strips. "The smell was the worst.

"I heard about how to make them stay dead before I left Philly. The involuntary nerve center," she touched the back of her own head and went back to tearing paper. He doubted she was even aware of what she was doing. "I saw on uBroadcast that you needed to destroy that part. That somehow after they died it was reactivated and made ...made them get up and walk around. And you have to take that part out. So they stay down. So they stay dead."

Out of napkin, she began tearing at the paper wrapper on the empty can of peaches. Her nervous fingers tore long thin strips as she talked about the people at her university, the long walk home, how she killed seven zombies and hid from a group of camo-clad men who had guns and crazy eyes.

"They always tell you they want to help you." She had run out of label and her hands rested on the wooden surface of the table. She shook her head, her curls bouncing. "But they don't. Not when there are a lot of them together. They go crazy." She drew a deep shuddering breath. "It's like they have to prove how powerful they are, and what better way than to stomp on the weak, people who don't have a chance against them? So you hide and stay away from them. Those fuckers, the ones that were chasing me today, jeez, they made me lose my pistol and my favorite crowbar." Judith exhaled, scattering torn paper onto the floor. "The worst are the kids. I only had to kill one, but that was enough."

He wanted to stop her, but someone knew that she needed to tell someone this, to let out the horror and despair.

"I killed a little kid." She spoke in a soft monotone. "At first I thought he was fine, he just looked lost. I asked him if he was okay. Then he opened his mouth and started groaning. That's a mind fuck right there, you know? Yeah, eventually a kid is

going to get infected, but to see it right there in front of you."
She closed her eyes, took a deep breath. "I smashed his head
and it exploded like a rotten little egg. I wanted to help him. I
didn't know..."

"That wasn't a kid, Judith. It wasn't a kid anymore."

"I know, but... it was still horrible. He looked so normal!"
She wiped at her nose. "When I finally got home, my mother
...my mother had shot my father and herself. I buried them in
the backyard." Judith put her face in her hands and burst into
tears.

"Jesus Christ," he said and he did go to her then and put his
arm around her. She sobbed against him, her arms circling
his neck. "Judith, relax, relax." Her tears were scalding hot
against his neck and he rubbed her back in a soothing, circular
motion. "Shhh. It'll be okay."

"It won't. It won't ever be okay again."

He held her until her sobs resolved into quiet hitches and
eventually silence. It was then that he realized that she had
fallen asleep. He continued to sit, not wanting to disturb her
sleep. Being here alone after burying her parents, she deserved
it.

****

Judith hated introspection, the navel gazing that led people
to philosophy, psychiatry and Prozac. She tried to be a realistic
practical type. She had done this so much that she wondered

if she could even access her emotions anymore, if there was still anything below the surface of zombie head bashing and dehydrated food.

But she had just collapsed in the arms of a complete stranger who had come along at the right time. His presence brought her pain to the surface, allowing her finally grieve for her parents, her missing brother and the life that she'd had before.

Now she was embarrassed because she had apparently also fallen asleep and drooled on the front of his shirt. *Nice. Real nice.*

Judith sat up, abruptly. "I am so sorry," she said, disentangling herself from him. Away from him, she felt chilled, even though the temperature inside the house must have been at least eighty degrees.

He touched her hair, his eyes sympathetic in the dim lantern light. "Jude, you were alone for a long time. It happens."

Avoiding his glance, she got to her feet and grabbed the empty can of peaches, dropped it in a plastic bag. "I'll take it out tomorrow, throw it over the wall. If you want to take that shower now, you can. Do you know how to work a camp shower?" She started to leave the room, then came back. "Also, there is a camp toilet on the back deck. It has a tent and it flushes. Come on, I'll show you around."

****

It was unbelievable how much a shower could change one's outlook on life. And fresh, clean clothes too, courtesy of Judith's brother Marcus, who had married and moved to Alabama, taking only one suitcase of clothes and leaving the rest, according to Judith. He dressed quickly, raked his hair back and was considering a shave when Judith knocked on the bedroom door.

"Everything okay?" She came up to his shoulder, so he would only have to bend a little to kiss her...and that was something he should really stop thinking about. "I'm getting ready to try to sleep."

"Thanks for everything," he said, rubbing his chin. "I might want a shave in the morning before I go."

Judith gazed at him for a long moment, her head titled to the side. "I guess we could talk about that in the morning."

He forced a laugh. "Talk about me wanting a shave?"

She walked away without answering him, went to her room and shut the door. He heard the sliding of heavy furniture and assumed she was using a barricade of some sort. Whether it was against a possible zombie invasion or just him, he didn't bother to think about. Instead, he closed his own door and tilted a chair under the doorknob. He knew his barricade was against possible zombie invasions.

CHAPTER SIX

The morning dawned hot and humid. Judith wished for rain as she washed up with the bucket of rainwater she'd obtained from the cistern on the third floor deck. The wind was kind today, the usual reek of decay was much less. She had to weed the garden today, then harvest and eat anything that had popped up in the last week. She was getting a little tired of fresh tomatoes, but by the time winter came, she would be wishing for them.

In the hallway, the floorboards creaked, startling her. Her automatic reaction was to reach for her gun until she remembered that she actually had a house guest. She rubbed the wet washcloth over her face in a slow circular motion, contemplating. It was nice to know that there was someone else in the house with her.

"Judith?"

"Be right out," she said, startled out of her reverie. She rinsed her washcloth and wrung it out, tossed it over the tower bar. She pulled her shirt over her head before she entered the hallway.

"Hi," she said.

He yawned. "Good morning."

Unlike her, he was shirtless in the late morning light. Judith couldn't help but take a moment to let her eyes roam freely over his bare chest and arms. In the light he looked much taller than he did last night and more than healthy. The muscles moved under his skin. Realizing she was staring, she flicked her eyes away, before he caught her staring...again.

"Are you hungry?" She struggled to keep her eyes from dipping below his waistband This wasn't the time to think about sex.

But she could be a good hostess.

"You can wash up. There's washcloths, towels and I left you a half bucket of water." She paused. "If you want to shave, there's razors and shaving cream under the sink. New."

"Thanks." Sky ran a hand across the short beard that obscured the bottom half of his face. "I'll be glad to get rid of this before I go."

Before I go. "You still only get a half bucket of water." His eyes, she now noticed, weren't brown like she thought, but a beautiful dark blue. He had the kind of looks that snuck up on you, with the long lashes, straight nose and surprisingly full lips that made her want to bite them. "I'm going downstairs and rehydrate some stuff to eat. When you come down, you can pick what you want."

As she walked past him he touched her arm, a brief brush that set her nerves jangling. He smelled like summer, fresh cut grass that stretched like a green, lush blanket under a hot afternoon sun.

"I just want to say I appreciate this. If it weren't for you, I'd be sleeping in a dirty bathroom somewhere." Those blue eyes were oh, so dreamy and sincere.

"Sure," she said, her fingers touching the spot where his fingers had made contact with her arm. "You saved me first though, so turnabout, fair play and all...." she let the sentence trail of as her eyes dropped to his lips again and scrambled to pick up her train of thought. "So, yeah. Stuff's in the bathroom, check out my brother's closet and come down to the first floor when you're ready."

* * * *

Judith sat at the dining room table eating what looked like grey library paste and reading a book. A few bottles of water and brown paper packets were scattered on the glossy cherry surface. Her brown eyes flicked over him when he sat down at the table, then widened at his new appearance.

"You look so much different!" She dropped her spoon in the plastic dish, a delighted smile breaking over her face. "You look younger."

Perhaps embarrassed by her outburst, she immediately picked her spoon and resumed eating. When she spoke again, her voice was politely neutral. "I hope you found everything you needed."

"I did, thanks." The packets were instant oatmeal, he realized. He had his choice of cinnamon apple, brown sugar, maple, and plain. "Oatmeal."

"Instant." Judith finished her meal before speaking, scraping the bowl for the last gluey bits. "This is only the tip of the iceberg, so take what you want. My parents were sort of hoarders. To be fair, they camped a lot too, but mostly they stored food." She waved her spoon. "Help yourself. Have one, two or all three." A tiny laugh escaped her. "They taste pretty much the same."

He chose the brown sugar, poured a half a bottle of water over the grainy powder, stirred and tasted it. It wasn't half bad, especially since he didn't have to eat it while looking over his shoulder. Being constantly on the lookout for zombies, killers and thieves could take the enjoyment out of eating.

Judith appeared to be reading but she was frowning slightly, as if she were thinking of something else more serious than the trials of the characters in *East of Eden,* the book she held.

He knew she'd hadn't slept well, judging by the tossing and turning he'd heard most of the night. She caught him studying her and raised her eyebrows. "Yes?"

"Did you sleep well?"

"Nightmares," she tossed off, marking her place with a slip of paper and closing the book. "As usual."

No longer frowning, she let her eyes roam over his face, down to his tattoos and back up again. "Science teacher, huh? Show me some science."

"What?" He wasn't sure what she was talking about.

"Some science! Show me what you taught." She clasped her hands on the table.

Sky stared at her, a smile tugging at the corner of his mouth. "You're serious."

"Yes." She made a hurry-up gesture with her hands, her corkscrew curls bouncing around her face and neck. "Teach me something about science."

He wracked his brain, recalling the tons of teacher workshops he'd had. "You got a plastic comb, some salt and pepper, a wool coat or sweater?"

She was back in a minute with what he needed and watched eagerly as he poured out the salt and pepper and mixed them together.

Sky brandished the black comb. "Now, with the magic of physics, I'm going to separate the pepper from the salt." He rubbed the comb on the red wool sweater then hovered it over the salt and pepper pile. The pepper pieces lifted out of the pile to attach themselves to the comb.

Judith actually clapped her hands together once, her eyes as bright as a child's. "Ooooo! How does that work? Did you just make a magnet? Is pepper metal? Do I sound like a total idiot?"

"It's basically the principle of positively charged and negatively charged electrons..." He explained to her the bare bones of static electricity, then showed her that if he held the comb close enough, it would pick up the salt too. "Lightning is a form of static electricity."

"Well," she said, still smiling. "I'd tell you something about history, but it wouldn't be anything you haven't heard on the History Channel. Maybe I should have been a science major."

The tone of her voice made him laugh. "It's fun now, but trying to teach it to a room full of teenagers? Yeah, not so much."

Judith gave him a long look. "That's the magic of teaching. It's not about what you know, but how you can show others." She got up from the table. "Let's go outside. I've gotta dump the trash and weed the garden." She picked up both plastic bowls and dropped them in a blue plastic bucket of water.

"Garden?" He helped her push the sideboard away from the back door.

"That's right, science teacher. We're going to study some botany."

* * * *

The backyard of Judith's house was nothing that he expected. The mainstay of the property was the tall concrete wall that surrounded the entire backyard on three sides. On one side of the house, there was a cast iron gate that guarded the cobblestone driveway that led to the garage.

Judith's garden was a medium sized patch of land where there were tomato plants, some strawberries and what looked like zucchinis. Rain catching cisterns lined the side of the garage, an optimal spot since there were no trees. The grass look liked it had been hacked down with a scythe or some other bladed instrument but was relatively neat, unlike the front yard. Sky turned in a circle, taking it all in. Given how most survivors were probably living, the gal had it all.

"Judith, this is amazing." The deck furniture was a dark green and looked comfortable..

"It is rather oasis-like, except for the occasional smelly breeze." She bent down, pulled a few errant weeds from around a strawberry plant. "It's safe too. The concrete walls keep people out and the gate is secure."

"It's secluded."

"Yes." She threw the bag of trash over her shoulder, waving off his attempts to carry it for her. "Follow me."

They walked, single file, down the hand mown path almost to the back of the property, where it divided into two paths. Judith took the left path and he followed. About twenty feet after the turn was a pit in the ground. Several white garbage bags were already there and she tossed hers in.

"Today is garbage day." She brushed her hands together, then stuck them in her jeans pockets, studied the white bags moving in the slight breeze. "Well, any day can be garbage day."

"What's down the path that goes to the right?" The sun was higher in the sky and beat down on his head. .

"My parents," she said shortly.

In the silence, he couldn't even hear a bird sing.

"Let's go back to the house, Jude." He had been calling her 'Jude' in his head since he'd found out her name and it just slipped out. "Judith," he corrected himself. "I gotta get packed and get on the road."

Brushing the hair out of her eyes, she turned to him. "You can call me Jude. I like it." She rolled her eyes. "So much better than Judy. I hated when people called me Judy. It's such a sitcom name." She started down the path back to the house. "And you can stay longer, if you can stand the company." Her words carried back to him over her shoulder. "I'm going to weed the garden now. You can help or you can sit on the deck."

"I'll help."

When they reached the garden patch, Jude cleared her throat. "Now it's my turn to teach you." She pointed. "Those are tomatoes. Hard to pull up a tomato plant now because not only are they large, they have tomatoes hanging off them. In fact, most of the plants are large enough that you can just get the tiny weeds. "

The several tomato plants that she had medium and small tomatoes hanging off of them. "Got it." He gestured at a plant with pointed jagged leaves, off in its own corner of the garden. Feigning ignorance, he asked, "How about that plant?"

"That?" She laughed. "That, my friend, is pot." She knelt on the ground, pulling small weeds from around the base of the larger, fruitful plants. She glanced up at him, giving him a view of the tops of her lovely breasts. "These weeds aren't going to pull themselves, teacher."

* * * *

Done with the garden and a quick lunch of tomatoes, saltines and strawberries, he happily accepted the water bottle that she offered him. Jude settled into a dark green chair next to his. "Now we rest after that field work." She winked, then leaned back and closed her eyes. "This is how things usually go around here. Not much entertainment."

Sky had taken the soda and the gum out of his pack and offered them to her, pleased at the way her eyes lit up at the cinnamon gum.

"Thank you," she said, shoving two pieces in her mouth at a time and chewing. "Jesus, that burns like hell." She blew out a cloud of cinnamon scented breath. "But I like it."

Being able to close your eyes without being on constant alert was a luxury that Sky hadn't experienced since he'd beaten his dead roommate with a bat. He leaned back into the cushions and relaxed, actually relaxed.

They lay there for a few minutes, each enjoying their thoughts.

"So," he said by way of conversation, "You're growing pot."

Jude opened those big brown eyes. "What?" She blinked. "Oh, just continuing what my parents legacy. My mother grew a lot of her own medicinal herbs." A sly smile crept across her face. "You interested?"

"Maybe."

"You're a bad teacher, aren't you?" She slid off the chair. "Come with me."

He followed back into the house and to the cellar. In a cubbyhole under the stairs, there were shelves lined with dark-colored screw top jars about six inches tall. Each was labeled with what it held.

The top three shelves - there were six in all - were different strains of marijuana.

"I...don't quite know what to say." He had never seen so much at one time. What he got came in a little slider bag and was mostly stems. But this was professional grade.

"It's good stuff, too." Jude laughed at the expression on his face. "Don't look so shocked, teacher. It's totally scientific, right, like botany?" She pressed her palms together, chest-height, in mock prayer. "Please don't send me to the principal's office."

He chuckled a bit. "Not me." He stuck his hands in his pockets and rocked on his heels. "You smoke?"

Jude let her mouth twist in a wry grin. "Do I look like a pot-tease to you?"

"Pot-tease....I like that. Especially the fact that you're not one."

Jude shut the door. "I have some upstairs. Wait for me on the deck."

* * * *

She emerged from the house with a wooden box. "It's grade-A stuff, totally organic."

The joint she extracted was rolled like he liked it, nice and tight and fully packed. Jude lit it took a huge hit and passed it to him.

"It's cherry."

He took the joint and sucked into the smoke, which hit him like a hammer. He leaned back against the cushions and gave her a lazy grin. "You're cherry."

Jude laughed and plopped down next to him on the sofa. "I mean cherry-flavored." She took the joint from him and took another hit. "Take it slow, Sky or it'll fuck you up with a quickness."

* * * *

Smoking was good for more than one thing. Sky sprawled on the cushions of the outdoor couch. It made you forget about zombies.

The setting sun striped the sky with a vivid palette of orange, violet and pink, a virtual paint box for anyone who cared to look. He stared, fascinated at the beauty of the colors, the end of the joint held in one hand and the warm, soft body of Jude snuggled against his side.

After a last drag, he stubbed out the roach in a ceramic ashtray that had seen its share of pot butts and slid his hands into Jude's prodigious amount of hair, gently rubbing her scalp until she sighed and lifted her head. She kissed him on the cheek.

"Hi, Sky." She smelled like strawberries and coconut and cherry marijuana smoke. Not a bad combination, considering. "You like the weed? It's nice, right?"

Yawning, he stroked her hair some more, rolled the tiny curls between his fingers.

"The weed's wicked, baby, but the company is even better." He watched those full lips of hers curve into a dreamy smile. He wondered if they tasted as good as they looked. He also wondered if she was going to let him find out. Her head was nestled in his lap and her T-shirt had pulled up to show the satiny skin of her belly.

Just one hand, he thought. He could lift it and place it ever so casually on her stomach.

"You're thinking so hard I can almost hear you. You're tense." Her hand drifted up to pat his face and fell back into her lap. The low timbre of her voice vibrated through him, revving him up. "Relax, Sky." She gestured at the horizon. "Watch the sunset."

With a great effort, he tore his eyes from that tempting strip of skin and watched the evening colors fade.

Jude shifted on his lap and sighed. "I'm hungry." She heaved herself up to a sitting, then a standing position, robbing him of her body heat. "Wow," she said, stretching. "That was something, wasn't it? How long have been sitting here?"

"Since after lunch, I think." Sky pushed himself up also. His throat was parched and he wanted to make sure that she didn't fall and crack her skull open, although he wasn't in the best shape himself.

"Come on." He stepped behind her through the sliding door that led to the kitchen. "We'll go out, hit the diner. Maybe get some White Castles."

"White Castle. If only," she said, opening a cabinet.

CHAPTER SEVEN

Smoking made her hungry. Jude rummaged through her bottomless cabinets until she found the box filled with clear plastic zip bags which were filled with dried fruit.

She stood up and brandished her find, suppressing a giggle at the blissed-out look on Sky's face. He leaned against the refrigerator, his gaze following her every move. "Apples, bananas and pineapples." Jude shook the bag. "You want?" *Because I could take a bite out of you.*

"No, thanks." He shook his head. "I had too many trail mix desserts when I was a kid. My mother was a health nut."

"A hippie health nut." She continued to rummage through the box. "She ruined you for life. Now I bet you've got a real sweet tooth, craving Ring Dings and sugary soda."

"Something like that." He grabbed a bottle of water, guzzled half of the warm liquid.

Jude watched him wipe his mouth, her mind telling her to be good, but her body, fueled by the pot, urging her to take advantage of the moment. She glanced around the kitchen. There was plenty of counter space available.

Behave yourself.

"Well." She snatched a bottle of water from the case that was sitting on the counter. "To the living room." Jude gave Sky a look as she walked past him. "If you can peel yourself off the refrigerator."

"I think I can manage."

"I present the formal living room." She waved a hand. "Enjoy the non-view."

He wandered around the room, touched the plywood over the window, ran his hand down the elaborate drapes that were still hanging. Jude pushed her shoulders back into the sofa cushions and dug into her bag of fruit, an attempt to distract herself from the growing awareness of her attraction to him. At first, it was nice just to have someone around. Now, her traitor body was trying to make her take a simple house-sharing to the next level.

And after only one day? It had to be the pot.

Neither of them spoke and the silence bore down on her ears. She opened the bag. "This is kind of my least favorite combination, but you make do, at least for now. Not like I can run to the store, right?" She laughed at her own joke.

"You could, but that's asking for trouble."

Jude glanced up at him. "That may be true, but if I hadn't gone to the store, I wouldn't have met you."

Over by the mantel, he nodded. He was looking at the family pictures she'd placed out one day when she was feeling low. If she could put the pictures out, then she could remember her family, remember what they looked like. She was terrified that as time went on, they would fade from her memory like a photograph left out in the sun.

"This is you?" Sky indicated a picture of her in pigtails, one sticking out wildly from her head, the other hanging in an orderly fashion. Yes, the hairdo was cockeyed, but it was her favorite grade school picture of herself.

"That's me, fifth grade."

"The braids are cute." He looked at her, then the picture, seeming to compare the two. "You haven't changed much."

She covered her embarrassment with a joke. "At least my hair doesn't look as bad." The sofa creaked as she moved around on it, working herself into a comfortable position among the cushions. "I could never keep my hair neat at school. I liked recess and gym too much."

"This your family?" He touched a wood-framed photo that was propped against a vase of long-dead flowers.

Jude nodded. "That's me and my brother and our parents on my college graduation day."

"Where's your brother now?

"Alabama? Texas?" She shrugged and popped a dried pineapple in her mouth. The sweetness of the fruit activated her saliva glands and she wiped a hand over the corner of her mouth before she continued. "Not long after that picture, he left med school, got married and left New Jersey. I told you that."

"You look very pretty." Sky settled beside her and stretched out his legs. "But I like the way you look now better."

Jude smiled and blinked her eyes coquettishly. "If I didn't know better, I'd think you were coming on to me."

Sky raised one shoulder. "You can take it any way you like."

Up close and personal, it was difficult to ignore his magnetism. And he smelled so good. And he was here, right here. She popped a banana chip in her mouth, preventing any foolishness from spilling out.

"Thank you," she said quietly.

"So your brother went to med school?"

"Yes," she said, relieved that the subject turned away from her. "My father was a doctor. He..." She let the sentence trail off.

"Tell me what happened," he said in a quiet voice and reached for her bag of fruit. He snagged a banana chip and ate it, crunched it between his teeth. "Not bad," he conceded. "Tell me what happened," he said again.

Jude swallowed the slick piece of apple she had in her mouth. "My father got infected at work. He worked for an infectious disease control company."

"Like the Center for Disease control?"

"It was a private company." She paused. "I am not really sure what he did, but it was a private company. He got infected." Jude dropped her snack, no longer interested in the sweet fruit. "He didn't know he was infected and he came home. And now they're both dead."

*

"They died two days before I got home."

"That's awful, Jude. I'm real sorry." It was an empty phrase, always had been, but he couldn't find anything else to say that this moment.

To his surprise, she shrugged, hitched her shoulders a little as she turned the banana chip in her fingers.

Every bit of concentration in her body was focused on the effort. "It is. Awful. But that's...how things are now, you know that. People, all the people you know, they're dead. People you meet, maybe they want to kill you for what you have. Or worse." She shivered a little and looked directly at him, her eyes narrowing slightly, delving into his conscience. "How many people that you knew before are dead now?"

He didn't think about it, tried not to think about it and didn't want to think about it now. But he would answer her questions. "My roommates. Probably my landlord. Teachers I worked with." He paused to consider the question further. "I don't really know."

"It's scary, isn't? So many dead in such a short period of time. And the world is like a jungle, survival of the fittest."

There was nothing to answer for this because she was right. The world was a jungle, with pockets of humanity in odd places, some too afraid to join forces with others because of distrust. You never knew who you were letting into your safe haven. People would kill for the set up that Jude had.

His hostess picked up her bag of fruit again. "So I said about a month because I stopped keeping track of the days after a while. What was the purpose?" Jude studied a banana chip and licked it before popping into her mouth, then slid the piece of dried fruit into her cheek, an unself-conscious gesture. The tropical smell of the dried fruit, the heat of the closed-in room and the proximity of her body to his. A perfect storm.

Desperately, he tried to think of other things to distract him from her presence not six inches away. *Pay attention to the conversation.*

He couldn't remember what she'd said, so he gave a generic agreeable answer. "Yeah, that's true."

He let his mind wander. Her breasts, for instance, full and soft under the cotton of her blue tank top. The glow of her skin in the lantern light, a sheen of perspiration giving it a gleaming luster. Her hair, the corkscrew strands bobbing around her face when she bent her head to the bag of fruit. Again, he started to wonder what she tasted like.

This is what happens when you get off the road and you feel relatively safe. You start thinking about things other than survival for a second. You start thinking about hamburgers, showers and good- looking women. Specifically, fucking a good-looking woman. And here she was, not an arm's length away. Hot. Sexy. And not even post-apocalyptic sexy, where you get so hungry that you'd ... eat anything. Not that. That messy hair, full lips and oddly optimistic attitude, they were working on him.

But he was a guest and you don't bang the woman who saved you from sleeping in a filthy abandoned house after having gum and shitty, cold canned food for dinner. Oh, and let's not forget the fact that you would have to clear the house of zombies by yourself and still not be sure that you're completely safe. You're on eggshells when she's given you the first real meal you've had in days. You should be on your hands and knees to her, thanking her and thinking of her as nothing but a kind sister, bringing you in from the figurative cold of the zombie infested streets.

"Sky?" Her voice jerked him out of the running conversation he was having with himself. Jude was staring at him now, a chunk of yellow pineapple held halfway to her mouth. "You alright?"

She flashed him a smile that kicked his simmering blood up another notch.

"Sorry, I was...daydreaming," he said. He sat up straighter on the cushions of the couch and tried to look more alert and less like he had a dirty movie running in his head. "What did you say?"

"I asked you what day it was. You must be spacing out from the pot." She gestured with the piece of fruit which was wet and shiny with what had to be her saliva. She must have had it in her mouth, sucking it between her lips. Maybe giving it a little lick, biting off a piece with her teeth.....he dragged his thoughts away from *that* and raised his wrist, squinted at his watch that he had liberated from some pawn shop in Irvington, along with the gun.

"It's Wednesday," he said and dropped his wrist in his lap. If he were still at work, it would have been an easy day, first through third periods free and only one duty period. They would be having turkey and stuffing in the cafeteria. Every Wednesday had been Thanksgiving Day.

Meanwhile, Jude stuck the pineapple chunk back in her mouth, sucked it and her fingers while she stared blankly at the boarded-up front windows, which still had their drapes. Sky followed her gaze, casually, to avoid watching her make love to that piece of fruit.

"Like it makes a damn bit of difference," she murmured and chewed and swallowed, wiping her hand on her jeans. She brushed her hair off the back of her neck and leaned back on the sofa cushions, took another swallow of her water. Sky listened as she hummed, but the sound was too quiet for him to pick up on the melody. Instead, he used the lull in conversation to study her more closely.

There was a beauty mark on her collarbone, the exact size and shape as if someone dipped a pencil eraser in black ink and touched it briefly to her skin. He wanted to touch it, to brush his fingers across to see if it would smudge.

"Where did you get your name?" She turned her head a little to the side, a brief frown creasing her brow as her eyes darted over his face. "Are you okay? You look all flushed. You want some water?" A giggle came from her. "You are fucked up."

Sky cleared his throat, knowing that his face was probably bright red even in the low light. "I'm fine." Once again, his brain scrambled to recall her question. "Ah, my mother liked the movie Guys and Dolls."

Her eyes lit up. "She named you after Sky Masterson?"

"Yeah."

"What's your middle name?"

"River."

"So your name is Sky River." She favored him with a wind chime laugh that settled into a grin. "Goes with the tattoos. Where are you from?"

"Tennessee," he said leaning back to be on eye level with her, paying attention to every detail.

"You told me that. Yes. What's in Tennessee?" Her eyes grew wide. "Elvis? And country music?" Enthusiasm shone in her eyes. "Do you live near Graceland?"

"Close enough, about an hour away, but I've never been."

"You've never been?"

He had to laugh at the look of shock on her face. "It's just a house, Jude."

"I guess." She extricated a banana chip and crunched it. He found himself slightly disappointed that she didn't lick it like she did the last one. "Do you think your parents are still alive?"

"Not sure. After everything started, I couldn't get in touch."

"But that's where you're going, right? You're on your way to find out?"

"Something like that."

Jude gave him a tiny grin, looked at him sideways. "You're very non committal, you know that?"

"I guess," he said and they both laughed.

Jude rolled the water bottle between her hands. Sky watched her do it, listened to the plastic crackling in the silence of the room. His heart beat too fast and he licked his lips.

He leaned over and brushed a curl out of her face. The tips of his fingers skimmed her damp temple and she shivered as if a cool breeze had drifted through the room. A steady pulse beat in her throat. He saw her shoulders moving up and down as she breathed, the small inhale/exhale movement causing her breasts to rise and fall. *It's the heat.* It twisted its steamy fingers around him, winding through his body straight to his groin. He was suddenly feverish, overwhelmed with a desire for this woman whom he had just met, a craving that he had been fighting since she'd crushed her body against his at their first meeting.

"Hey, Jude." Sky slid his arm around her waist and pulled her against him, nearly onto his lap. The water bottle dropped from her hands, making a barely audible clunk on the rug below. His lips found hers in an urgent, hungry kiss. He marveled her sweet taste.

Jude wrapped her arms around his neck with an eagerness that surprised him, crushing her breasts against his chest. The flick and flutter of her tongue against his drove him into such frenzy that his dick was straining painfully against the fly of his jeans. He tightened his arms around her, pressing her more firmly against him. She moaned softly against his lips, the seductive vibrations stoking his lust even higher. The tangy flavor of the fruit she'd been eating filled his mouth and her warm summer scent intoxicated him.

Breaking apart, for a moment, they stared at each other, their ragged breath splitting the silence of the tomb quiet room.

"I want you to fuck me, make me forget all this shit, okay?" She kissed him, her tongue sliding against his with passion-fueled aggression. "Okay?"

"Yes." Telling her no was not an option. "Take this off." He grabbed the hem of her tank and yanked it over her head, breaking the contact of their mouths only to allow the cotton material to pass between them.

He pressed his face to the smooth, fragrant skin of her breasts that pulled the fabric of her bra tight. Everything about her was exquisite, perfect, wonderful.

Straddling him, she ground against his trapped erection, sank her teeth into the tender flesh of his neck, his lip and finally his earlobe. Her kisses were greedy and savage, excitement obvious in their ferocity.

Sky bit into the soft flesh above the cup of her bra. A low sound, half sigh, half moan, carried to his ears, urging him on. The floral scent of her hair, the taste of her mouth and the incessant pressure of her weight on his lap was nearly unbearable. Forget going south. They could stay here together while he fucked her into forgetting what was happening outside the four walls. *Yes.* His feverish mind closed to any other possibility than being right here, right now.

Her hips traced a slow, burning swirl against him, making his ears ring and his legs tremble.

"Sky," she breathed against his ear and hot desire raced through him. He grasped her bottom with both hands, drawing her closer.

The glow of the battery powered lantern illuminated her face only slightly, but it was enough for him to see her eyes fastened on him as she unhooked her bra and drew his hands to her naked, luscious breasts. He kissed her long and hard, stroking the soft skin, then kneading her tight nipples between his fingers. She moaned into his mouth and raked her fingers through his hair.

He sucked a taut nipple into his mouth, eliciting a tiny cry of pleasure from her and increasing the pressure against his dick, which was now aching with raw, brutal desire. If she continued to grind against him like that, he would burst. Right in his pants.

His mouth released her breast with a small "pop" only fasten upon the other, flicking his tongue across the tight bud until her back arched and she moaned in pure rapture, her body writhing against his.

"Oh, don't stop, please..." She inhaled and dug her fingers into his shoulders. He fumbled at the button on her jeans wanting to get them off and out of the way. To pleasure her like he wanted, like he *needed* to, to hear her call out in ecstasy.

In the space between their breathing, there was a distinct thump outside, then a sliding sound, as if there was something dragging against the wooden shingles of the house.

Chapter Eight

"Oh, no, no." Jude groaned as she hurried to gather her clothes. She felt like she was moving in slow motion as she dressed, the last tendrils of arousal draining from her body. It took her two tries to hook her bra because her hands were shaking from the adrenaline that was now surging through her system. That noise could only mean one thing.

She yanked her clothes on as Sky grabbed his bat.

"Just leave it," she said. "Don't go out there." Her stomach rolled at the prospect of either of them going outside. It was dark and who knew what that sound was? Anything could be out there.

"When there's one, there will be more, Jude." He knelt down, checked something in his boot. He stood up. "You gotta get rid of them while you can, or else..."

His mouth snapped shut over his words when there was another thump accompanied by a low, weak groan.

Jude's eyes stretched wide and Sky's arms pebbled into goose bumps, even as he kept his face void of expression. He was just as scared as she was. There were only reluctant heroes or plain crazy people. She sank down on the patterned rug and put her hands over her face, the mantra beginning in her head. She couldn't go out there, she wouldn't go out there. And she wasn't going to let the only civilized human being she had seen in weeks go out there either.

"They'll go away, Sky, they will." She pulled her knees to her chest and wrapped her arms around her legs, fought to keep from rocking back and forth. "Please don't go. Don't go out there."

"Have to. They'll draw more, Jude. If there's too many, we'll be trapped." He tapped the head of the bat on the rug, his gaze far away. "I need your help."

"No." She refused to meet his eyes, dark and pleading. She didn't care if they surrounded the damn house.

"They could be anywhere."

"Not in the backyard. They can't get in the backyard. The gate, remember?"

They both winced at a soft bumping sound that morphed into a dragging sound. Sky turned and looked at the wall from where the sound came, as if he could see through it.

"You have to." The tone of his voice did not change, but behind the calm, she heard steely determination. "When there's one, others will come. They'll take over the front yard, start pressing against the door, the gate.."

Jude clapped her hands over her ears. "Shut up," she whispered. "Shut up!"

But even her hands over her ears didn't stop the thumps of bodies contacting the house. There were surely more than one, those things were bumping against the house. Bumping and sliding, like a drunk who can only keep his inebriated world from tipping by bracing himself against something solid as he walks. Jude shivered. Those weren't drunks out there. She squeezed her arms more tightly around her tucked-up legs. Right now, she hated Sky. *Hated him.* He wanted her to go out and face those walking corpses.

Who does that to someone they like? Two minutes ago, he was kissing her like they were the only two people in the world and now.... She couldn't even look at the cold, hard look on his face.

"I might know them," she said now, biting back the bitter words she wanted to say. "They might be my neighbors."

"Highly doubtful. Your neighbors are either gone or trapped in their house." He gave her a look, which she studiously ignored.

The sounds creeped her out: it was as if there were a thousand whispers outside, all of them calling her name.

"Jude." He paused. "You're not a coward. Be afraid, but don't be a coward."

"Sounds like some bullshit you'd say to your students." *You fucking bastard,* she thought without malice. Appealing to her sense of courage 'had been the right tactic. She hadn't survived for the past weeks by being afraid. Killing zombies was nothing she hadn't done before. At least now she had company.

"Because it works." He grabbed her arm and she allowed him to pull her up, thinking she might as well die this way as in any other. "The plan is simple. You open the door, let me go out, you guard the door. If there are only a few, I'll take care of them. Don't want any of them slipping in while we're both out there."

What he said did make sense, but Jude wanted to be sure of the numbers. "Hold on." She crossed to the window and peeked through a crack between the boards. The weak moonlight shone on three shuffling forms in the driveway. "There's three." Her skin crawled at the low groaning sounds they made and wondered how they found their way to the house.

"Easy as cherry pie, Jude." He hefted the bat to his shoulder. "Nothing we haven't done before."

A little jolt of pleasure went through her at the sound of the "we". There hadn't been a "we" that included her in a long, long time.

"Wait a second." Jude went to the dining room and retrieved her crowbar, stuck it in a loop on her belt. Back in the living room, she stuck her hand under the sofa and pulled out a rifle.

Sky stared at her for a moment, then, a smile broke across his face. "You are a goddess, Jude. Where the hell did you get all this firepower?" He reached for the gun. "But you shouldn't use it. Too much noise."

Jude held it out of his reach. "This one's mine." She winked. "This Gamo Big Cat is quiet as a kitty's purr."

"You a good shot?" He gave her the once over.

"I am, thank you very much. Four years in the college rifle club."

Sky burst out laughing. "Jude, baby, you're full of surprises." He seemed genuinely delighted with her and she flushed with pleasure.

She flushed even more when he closed the space between him and kissed her, holding her body tightly against his. When he let her go, they were both breathing hard.

"Stay on the porch, " he said. "Keep an eye on any coming round the side of the house."

"There's a fence," Jude told him. "No backyard access."

"That helps." He thought for a moment. "But I want you to stay on the porch. I need you to cover my back just in case, okay?"

Jude nodded, fear bubbling in her stomach. She reached for the door but then stopped.

"Kiss me again," she said.

He obliged. It was a softer kiss this time, one that warmed her body and left her tingling.

Jude leaned her gun against the wall and wound her hair in a tight knot. Didn't want any zombies grabbing hold. She put one hand on the doorknob.

He kissed the back of her neck, the bat in his left hand. "Ready, Freddy?" he whispered the question.

"I wish Freddy were going instead of us," she said and pulled open the front door.

* * * *

Jude's nose wrinkled at the smell. It wasn't so bad inside, where she used dried lemongrass and essential oils to keep the air somewhat breathable but outside, breathing the fetid turned the term "fresh air" inside out.

There were three of them, which meant that there would be more. Though brain dead, they seemed to send out some sort of signal to the others. If a few gathered in one place, then it was a given that the numbers would soon increase, that is if you didn't put them down and quick.

Sky was right, damn him.

While Sky went down the front steps, Jude walked to the end of the wooden porch that overlooked the driveway. The shambling wrecks patrolled the long length of blacktop, bumping shoulders as they passed each other, veering only slightly off course before they realigned themselves.

The male one wore a tattered t shirt and jeans and looked near rotted, but its milky eyes were vivid and alive with malice. Jude winced at the chopping sound of its jaws as Sky approached him. She watched as he swung the bat, heard the hollow clunk when wood connected with skull.

Jude set her sights on the second one, about twenty five feet farther down the driveway. Fuck the noise, she was going to spray this one all over the driveway.

"Pull," she whispered and disengaged the safety, a wide grin on her face.

The crack of the rifle ripped through the silence of the night and the zombie's head disintegrated.

"Jesus, Jude!" Sky stage whispered to her. "I told you about that gun."

"Sorry," she said, still grinning. It felt good to shoot them.

"A little warning next time. Almost made me piss my pants." He approached the third one and swung, his biceps bulging against the sleeves of his t-shirt. Another *thunk* and the thing's head exploded, yellowish-gray and black goop flying. "Christ, that's disgusting."

The matter of fact tone of his voice carried clearly to Jude, who laughed. "Come inside." With the gun in one hand and her crowbar tucked thumping against her leg, she turned and retraced her steps to the front door.

"I think that's it." His voice came to her clearly across the short distance. "Three down and—shit!"

The fourth one must have come from the bushes that lined the drive. As Jude watched in horror, the zombie slammed into Sky, knocking him to the ground and the bat out of his hand.

The rifle was useless with the two bodies tangled together. She couldn't shoot the zombie without shooting Sky. She pulled the crowbar out of the loop on her belt and swallowed hard as she stepped off the porch, only to have a claw latch onto her arm.

* * * *

It had his left foot now and Sky was glad for the heavy hiking boots he wore. He kicked at it, but the thing was tenacious, using the hold on his leg to gradually make its way up to the exposed flesh of his stomach.

He gave a great heave backwards, digging his heels into the blacktop an attempt to get away from the stinking hunk of flesh.

The asphalt scraped the skin on his back and he winced.

If that wasn't bad enough, he heard Jude scream. *Fuck.*

He had brought them both out here to die.

Sky stretched his arm out, fingers reaching for the bat that lay just out of reach, to no avail. The zombie was too heavy and he could make no progress.

The knife.

He drew up his right foot and withdrew his switchblade from his boot. *Back of the head.* He pushed the button that deployed the stiletto's blade, eight inches of tempered steel that was illegal in most states. Grimacing against the horrible smell, he slid the eight inches into the side of the creature's neck and yanked it upward. Lucky for him, the zombie was rotted enough that going through the flesh went as easy as a hot knife through butter. Black liquid poured out.

To his relief, the zombie went limp and released the death grip on his foot. He kicked the body aside and he reached for the bat, using it to push himself off the ground and limped toward the house, searching for Jude.

CHAPTER NINE

When the zombie grabbed her arm, Jude struck out blindly. The raspy touch on her skin gave her the willies. The first swing bounced off the zombie's arm, effectively separating its hand from her. Jude backed up, raised the crowbar and smashed it in the zombie's neck.

It fell to the ground, body still twitching, reaching for her. She hacked at it again, little whines coming from her throat as she beat the thing's head to a pulp. *Stay dead!* Her arm hurt, but she kept swinging.

"Jude." Sky put his hand on her shoulder, shaking her from her trance. "Let's go in."

Once inside, he helped her push the table across the door as neither of them spoke. He felt her eyes on him as he unhooked the holster from his jeans and tossed it on the table. He was drained and shaky. What he wanted was a drink from one of those bottles he'd seen in the kitchen and another joint. He turned to Jude to suggest this only to find that he was looking down the barrel of her rifle.

"Were you bitten?" The barrel of the gun was aimed at his face. Despite everything that had happened, he'd never had the dubious pleasure of a gun pointed at him.

As he stared at her, he could see the barrel of the gun shake slightly, but her eyes were steady. At this range, she'd blow him all over the fucking wall.

"Jude, no, I'm not bit." He held up his arms. "Put the gun down."

She shook her head. "No." Her hair had loosened from its knot and floated around her face. She may have looked like an angel, but her eyes did not waver. "Take off your clothes."

"What?"

Jude gave him a look of exasperation. "You heard me. Take off your clothes so I can see."

His eyes flicked to his gun, lying on the dining room table. If he could--

"You won't make it," she sing-songed. "Would you rather be naked or dead? Take off your clothes. Please," she added.

Jude smiled at him so sweetly over the barrel of the gun that he couldn't believe that this was happening. Resigned, he unlaced his boots and slid out of them, his bloodied jeans and his t-shirt, leaving him only in boxer briefs.

"Nice," she said, keeping the gun on him. The barrel was beginning to shake a little and he knew it was costing her some effort to hold it steady. She raised her eyebrows. "Turn around, please."

He followed her directive, trying not to think. His lower back burned from scraping it on the driveway, but all the zombie blood had dribbled onto the driveway, not him.

*

"Your back is all abraded," she said. "But otherwise, very nice, again." She could see where he had scraped his back against the driveway, but beyond that, he seemed whole. Satisfied that he was bite free, Jude motioned with the gun. "You can put your clothes back on. If you want."

"Are you going to hold me at gunpoint until I do?" Sky slid back into his pants, zipped them but didn't button them. They hung low on his hips, exposing the waistband of his underwear. "We're not going to go through this again, Jude. You're going to have to trust me a little more."

"Trust you? I've only known you for one day. Barely one day." Jude took a deep breath, her finger curling in the trigger guard. *Trust him.* It had been a mistake, inviting him back here. Should have given him a quick thank you and left him to fend for himself. Instead she'd gone soft and mushy, desperate for human company. If she shot him now, she wouldn't have to worry about him getting killed. Better now than later, after she got too attached. There would be no risk of him turning into a zombie. She'd blow his head clean off, just like in the movies. Jude raised the gun, a little higher, her finger tightening against the trigger.

"If I shoot you, I won't have to trust you, right?"

His expression relaxed, moved from anxiety to serenity, as if he were used to being confronted with death. "You're not going to shoot me, Jude." His voice was low, crooning. "Not going to happen. Because you know me."

"I don't know you." She hardened herself against that charming smile of his, the little creases at the corners of those dark blue eyes. Her arms were shaking. Five pounds of rifle now seemed more like twenty.

Jude jerked the gun back up when he began walking toward her. "Stay there," she ordered. She gnawed at her lip, confused thoughts running through her brain. Being with someone, having them around, meant she would be responsible for them in some way. She didn't want anyone to have to make the choice that her mother made.

Okay, she wouldn't shoot him, but he had to go, he had to leave. "I want you to pack up and go when it gets light enough." He was a liability, a burden. She refused to get attached to someone else who could be dead tomorrow.

"Put the gun down, Judith." He took another step toward her, his eyes on hers.

She tore her eyes away from his sympathetic ones, focused instead on the area in the center of his chest.

One in the chest, then in the head. *Double tap.* "I'll shoot you," she groaned. *Why wouldn't he stop?* "I'll do it." A trickle of sweat ran down her back and her lungs worked convulsively to bring oxygen to her body. It was too hot.

He shook his head, once. "No, you won't."

She blinked against unexpected tears. "I won't shoot, but you have to go, okay? You can't stay here anymore." Her whole body trembled with the effort of holding the gun and a tear slipped down her cheek. "Promise me, you'll go. It'll be better for the both of us. "

"It won't be."

Close enough to touch. If she pulled the trigger now, she'd vaporize him.

Sky reached out and placed his hand on the barrel, nudged it toward the floor. Her finger slipped out of the trigger as his hand slid over hers, disengaging her shaky, sweaty grip. He took the gun from her and placed it in the corner.

*

He was too close, crowding her space, but she couldn't help but take in the smell of his bare skin, feel the whisper of his hands against her face and his mouth brushing across her throat, then his lips pressing against hers. The emotions roiled within her, making her mind reel with confusing thoughts. Despite her conflicting thoughts and the sheer implausibility of the situation, she was unable to keep herself from responding.

Jude laced her arms around his neck, violently pulling him against her, the surging excitement intensifying. Every ounce of her being strained toward him, her stomach fluttering with growing anticipation. She slid her tongue against his, the heat in her pussy blooming into an insistent, itchy ache, an appetite that demanded attention. His erection pressed in the vee of her thighs and she moaned with unabashed lust, grinding herself against him, feeling the heat of his bare skin under her hands.

He teased and grazed the skin of her throat with his teeth, biting at the bared skin of her shoulders. Jude gasped at the sensation of his teeth against her skin.

Sky peeled her tank top off and tossed it to the side. Then he was kissing her again, sucking and biting at her lips. She closed her eyes, letting the carnal feelings sweep her away. She rubbed against him, the promise of his erection teasing her.

"You taste so good," he murmured as he unzipped her jeans and peeled them down her legs, making short work of her boot laces. She wriggled out of boots and jeans as one, kicking until she had extricated herself from the tangle.

Sky gazed at her as he exhaled a long, slow breath, his eyes filled with a longing that made her shiver, despite the heat. One hand reached out to nudge one bra strap down her shoulder, his hand barely brushing her skin.

His eyes flicked up to hers, his expression a mix of admiration and lust and something else. "You're so...." he paused, as if searching for the right words. Instead of completing his thought, he knelt in front of her, smoothing his hands up her legs as he kissed her thighs, nipping gently at the sensitive flesh. Moving upward, he pressed his lips to the small swell between her navel and the narrow waistband of her panties. He stood and in a swift movement, he lifted her onto the dark wood sideboard that stood next to the door.

Jude braced herself on the lacquered surface, the back of her thighs sticking to the smooth wood as he brushed his hands over her stomach and arms, the ticklish, yet arousing touch of his fingers against her skin almost too much to bear. Her every nerve ending jangled with delicious sensation, each skin to skin contact making her crave him more.

"Sky," she whispered, touching him everywhere she could reach, running her hands across the hard muscles in his shoulders and back, rubbing her fingers through the softness of his hair.

He trailed kisses along her upper chest, each press of his lips leaving a heated brand against her skin, distracting her as he deftly unhooked her bra and slid it from her body. Jude arched her back, hands splayed across the bare expanse of his back and thought about nothing but his skin against hers. Everything she cared about in that moment was narrowed down to this small part of her universe.

When he sucked at her nipples, drawing first one hard peak into his mouth, circling it with the wet heat of his lips and tongue, then doing the same with the other, Jude let out a small cry of desperation. She pressed her head against the wall, cradling his head in her hands, her pussy humming with such urgency that every nerve in her body sang with need. Need for him to touch her, lick her, fuck her, anything that would give her some relief.

Pressing her thighs together in a futile bid for some relief, she fumbled at his zipper and slid her hands past the light spray of hair on his belly to wrap her hand around his cock.

Sky made a noise in this throat, midway between a sigh and a grunt when she squeezed and stroked the firm, warm flesh. Touching him, feeling the size of him increased her excitement as she anticipated him inside her.

"Slow down," he mumbled against her neck, placing his hand on hers, stilling her rhythm.

"No," she mumbled, hooking her fingers in her panties and shimmying them down her hips. She wrapped her arms around his neck for another delicious, body-heating kiss, sucking his bottom lip into her mouth and nipping at it. His hand went to where she wanted it, *needed* it the most when his fingers delved into her slick folds, stroking her clit until her whole body trembled with ecstasy from the intense sensation.

"Do you want more?" His tongue touched the tip of her earlobe, then he bit the soft flesh softly, his entire body stiff with arousal.

"I want this," she pulled out his cock and stroked it with both hands. "Now who's the tease?"

With a smothered laugh, he pulled her forward and entered her with one smooth thrust.

Her heart raced as her body adjusted to the feeling of being filled even as she hissed out breath between her teeth.

"Oh, Jude," he sighed against the curve of her neck. "Is that..."

"It's fine, it's good, keep going, please..." she gasped, eyes tightly closed against the exquisite feeling.

She tilted her hips, a slight movement upward and hooked her legs around his waist. The early morning heat raised sweat on their joined bodies as Jude pressed her face into Sky's shoulder and held on as he drove into her, the momentum of his thrusts banging the sideboard against the wall. She let her mind shut down and allowed exquisite sensation to take over, blurring out the insanity of the real world around them.

*

Sky kissed her neck and breasts as he moved within her, fighting to retain control as her inner muscles gripped and squeezed his cock. She was so tight and so incredibly hot that he had to bite his lip to keep himself from shooting off right then. Adjusting his too-frantic rhythm, he focused on giving her as much pleasure as possible.

She watched him through half-closed eyes. Her hands moved over his upper body, brushing here, stroking there and but especially careful against his scraped lower back. Her hair had loosened from its knot and blossomed around her head, the light brown curls a bronze highlight against the bland white of the wall behind her.

"Oh, Sky." She brushed her fingers across the side of his head, across his cheek. "That's good."

"Good," he managed.

She kissed him, a soft kiss that ended with a sigh. "Yes, that's it...Oh!" Then he felt it, felt her, a rhythmic squeezing and releasing of pressure around his cock that sent a jolt of pure, white sensation up his spine. She bit his shoulder as she came, her body rigid against his.

After that, he didn't know what she did, just that with a shifting of her hips and a slight adjustment of her legs, she was even tighter. The sensation drove him faster toward the edge and before he realized what was happening, he came in a series of short, rushing spasms that surprised him with their intensity.

They started at each other for a brief moment before Sky drew her to him and kissed her tenderly, winding both hands through her hair, then pressing his forehead to hers. Worry shone in her eyes as she tried to pull away but he held her steady.

"Hey," he said. "Come on." He helped her down from the table, zipped his pants and gathered her clothes. "Let's get some sleep."

CHAPTER TEN

J udith slipped into sleep easily but her dreams were black nightmares, where her friends turned to zombies before her eyes and reached out for her, chasing her. At the end of the dream, she had buried her parents but the next morning when she woke up the mounds of dirt were moving and undulating as if something were under the surface trying to get out, to get at her.

She had trained herself to not scream out, even as the nightmare unreeled behind her twitching eyelids, but she must have made some small distressed sound because when she awoke, Sky was rubbing her shoulders and the noontime sun shone through the second story windows. The pungent smell of pot tickled her nose.

"You had a bad dream, Jude. Here." He passed her the joint and she took a long, cleansing pull, passed it back to him. His eyes were reddish as if he had been up all night or been smoking pot all night or both. Probably both.

"It's all a bad dream, Sky." She scrubbed her hands over her face. "This whole life...it's just about waiting for the end of the road." She sat up and rubbed her face with her hands, then rooted around in the bed clothes until she found a t-shirt and slipped it on. "And there's way more where that came from." She indicated the joint. "There's a whole other stash."

"Judy-Jude, there's no end of the road when you're with me. Remember that." He laced his fingers through her tangled hair and kissed her long and slow, sending the shivery tingly feeling all over her.

"You taste like pot," she told him and giggled, the effects of the joint traveling through her body, making her head light and airy. "And cherries."

"You too, baby," he said and kissed her again, sucking at her lips and tongue until she thought she would burst with delight. She was overwhelmed with an urge to touch herself, to slide her fingers between her legs and bring herself off while he kissed her like that.

"Whoa," she breathed when he released her. She lay back on the pillows, knowing an idiotic smile was pasted on her face.

Her lips tingled with the influx of blood and she closed her eyes for a moment to better savor the feeling.

After a moment, she opened her eyes to scrutinize him. "That sheet is not decent."

"So you're telling me to put some clothes on." He sucked on the joint, held it to her lips, for a last toke, then stubbed it out in the ashtray on the bedside table. "I've taken off and put on clothes more times in the last twelve hours for you than I've done for any woman."

Jude giggled, feeling giddy and light. "I'm just stating a fact. Far be it from me to insist that anyone put on any clothes." She eased off the bed and went to the closet where she grabbed two bottles of water.

"Is there anywhere you don't have supplies?"

Turning to face him, a water bottle in each hand, she pretended to ponder the question. "Well, there's only a gun and some water in the bathroom, so, there you go."

She walked to the bed and handed him a bottle and twisted the cap off of hers, sipped at the tepid water. "I miss cold stuff. And ice. I would love some ice."

Sky sat up next to her, the sheet pooling around his waist. His hair stuck up in all directions on his head and the arm tattoos were more vivid against his skin in the morning light.

"You really went all out with the tattoos." She reached over and ran her fingers over the designs.

He leaned against the headboard. "Seemed like a good idea at the time. Hurt like hell, though." He rubbed his shoulders against the cloth. "Like my back."

"Hold on a second," she said and left the room. She retrieved a can of first aid spray from the bathroom and re-entered the bedroom, shaking the can.

"Turn over." She shook the can. "It's antibacterial spray. For your back."

His eyes squinted up. "That's going to burn."

"No worse than those tattoos. Turn over."

"But I wanted the tattoos. I paid for them. That's not really a good analogy, Jude."

"What do you know about analogies, you're a science teacher. Turn over." She arched an eyebrow and put a hand on her hip. "And if it makes you feel better you can pay me." *He was being impossible.* "Stop being such a baby. Turn over."

After giving her a look that was half reproachful, half sorrowful, he turned over onto his stomach. Jude inched the sheet down until all the abrasions were uncovered, unable to resist running her hand across his skin.

Occasional dark brown freckles dotted his back and arms and she planted a kiss on an especially dark one near his shoulder blade. She smiled to herself as she shook the spray.

"Tell me before you spray, Jude." His voice was partially muffled by the pillow.

"I will." She popped the top off. "I took the top off." Smiling evilly, she sprayed the abraded area liberally, laughing when he yelped at the sudden sting. "And that's me spraying."

He turned over and grabbed at her, the sheet dangerously close to slipping past the point of no return.

Jude jumped on top of him, pinning him to the mattress. "Now I'm going to have to do it again because you rubbed it all off."

He grabbed her wrist, shook it and the can of spray dropped to the rug. "No more torture, I can't take it."

"Aww, come on," Jude bent to kiss him on the lips. "I was just starting to have fun."

"You're an odd gal, Jude," he said, pulling the sheets from between them until they were skin to skin. "But I think I like you." He reached under her the loose t shirt, rubbed her nipple until her eyes closed partway and she shifted her hips against him.

She felt him stiffening between her legs. "Oh, goody," she said quietly. "The ride's open."

****

"When did you get them? How old were you?" She let her fingers trace the twisting dark lines that ran along his arms. *Very goth.* She passed the joint to him and he took it, inhaling the fragrant herb deeply before placing it in the ashtray.

"Fifteen."

Jude raised her eyebrows. . "Your parents let you do that?" Her parents had disapproved of tattoos, saying they were only fit for people who either rode motorcycles or who went to prison. Meanwhile, they had their own little pot farm going in the garage.

He smiled a little. "She encouraged me to express myself."

Jude laughed. "Express yourself, indeed. They must be very liberal."

"I guess." His eyes were thoughtful for a second.

There was a brief silence and Jude fervently hoped that they were alright. She squeezed his forearm.

"I'm sure they're fine."

He didn't answer and Jude didn't press further.

"It's going to be a hot day." He broke the silence between them. "Better get those bodies in the front moved away from the house."

"Mmmm," was all she said. Enough time to think about garbage disposal later. "Tell me more about your teaching life. The students must have been tough."

"Yeah. And some of them didn't make it."

"Make it?"

"Got pregnant, left school to work or take care of family members, got shot." He shrugged, the muscles of his shoulders making the movement a thing of grace. Jude hid a grin. It took a zombie apocalypse for her to find someone she really liked and who was hot to boot. She reached out and traced a line down his belly, swirling her finger around his navel. He grabbed her hand.

"That tickles."

"You're very sensitive. How long did you teach?"

"Five years."

"So you kept going back?"

"I did. "

"Why?" Jude turned the full force of her gaze on him. "Why did you stay?"

He drew air into his lungs and didn't answer. She thought he wouldn't until he finally said, "I left home when I was sixteen years old. My mother had remarried and her new husband didn't take too well to a sixteen year old who wasn't his. Truth be told, I didn't take too well to him either. I gave him a lot of problems."

"As teenagers do."

"He gave my mother a lot of shit about me. I always heard them arguing and her crying. So, long story short, I decided that I should get out, give them both some peace."

"But they would be worried about you!" Jude was aghast. How could a teenager take care of himself? "Weren't you worried about them being worried?"

"Only my mom." He blew out his breath. "I ended up renting a room in some boarding house and working at a grocery store. Didn't go too far, just the next town over. So, I've been gone a couple weeks or so and I'm working the register and my baseball coach and math teacher comes in.

"He wants to know what happened, and all that crap. I tell him, and next thing I know, he gives me a place to stay and I finish my last two years of school. Ended up going to Rutgers on scholarship. Then I got involved in the Astronomy Files, a program that brings sciences to schools and I started to like the idea of working with kids."

Jude stared at him. All she had wanted to do was work in a museum back room where she could get away from people. Sky, on the other hand, had jumped right in the middle of a potentially dangerous situation and kept going back. That was much more than she had ever done.

"That's brave. "

"I wouldn't exactly say brave. It's just what happened."

Jude rolled her half-clothed body against him. "I'm glad you happened to me."

He hugged her to him, and kissed her shoulder, his stubble sandy against her skin. "Likewise, Jude."

CHAPTER ELEVEN

L ater on that day, Sky disposed of the zombie corpses under a hot afternoon sun while Jude stood watch with her rifle and crowbar tucked into her belt. He dragged the bodies to the lawn of the house across the street, ears and eyes on high alert for any stray movement or sound. After dumping the last one, he turned toward the house, a quaint looking brick ranch with a wild tangle of black-eyed Susans growing directly under the picture window.

Up the street, Jude stood on the lawn a couple hundred feet away. She faced in the opposite direction for now, watching for any stray zombies or people. He stepped closer to the flowerbed, his boot making a deep impression in the soft, dark soil, meaning to pinch a few of the vivid orange and brown flowers.

He had broken off three of blooms when there was a soft thump against the picture window not two feet in front of him. Sky glanced up at the sound and saw a bloated gray face, half covered by the ragged pink curtains, starting back at him through the glass. There was something off about it and it took him a moment before he realized that the cheek was hollowed out, the flesh stripped away and he could clearly see the whitish jawbone working up and down behind the glass like some macabre marionette. His legs froze and he could only stare, rooted to the ground by the horrific sight.

I wonder how strong that glass is?

The apparition thumped on the glass again, its bony fingers scrabbling against the glass in a futile attempt to get to him. The curtains flapped around the walking corpse and Sky could only imagine what the inside of that house must smell like. The creature banged on the glass again, and somehow he knew he had to move, to get away before the thing broke through the window and chased after him. But all he could do was stand and stare.

"Sky," Jude's clear voice carried over the quiet distance. "Come on, now. Let's get back inside. That's the Campbells' house. I don't think they ever got out."

It was only her voice that loosened his frozen limbs, and he was finally able to back away from the window, squeezing the flowers in a tight fist. If only he were dead, really dead, he wouldn't have to be faced with all this.

* * * *

Jude was asleep and the world outside held its usual tomb silence. Sky fiddled with the short wave radio, thinking how much noise there had been outside his apartment in Hillside. There were always cars going by, sometimes blaring the radio, the heavy bass beat penetrating the walls of the house he shared, driving him nuts. The place had been cheap and clean and relatively safe, but the noise was often too much.

He would love to have the people, the traffic sounds, all of that back. Noise was comforting. It let him know that there were other human beings alive and around. The dead silence made him want to bang things around just to make sure he was still alive.

From the radio he got mostly static and weird electronic noises that never developed into anything. He found a quiet area on the dial and left the radio on in the hopes that something would come through.

Jude had tons of everything, food, books, batteries, paper goods, liquor and pot. She also had a good stash of painkillers and antibiotics for "just in case", as she put it. He sat down on the sofa and opened one of the books he'd began reading a few days ago. *The Lion, the Witch and the Wardrobe.*

He had only read about five or so pages when Jude came downstairs, shaking her hair out. She was too thin; she was eating less and less every day despite the pot smoking and at this point she was down to a handful of dry cereal in the morning, some dried fruit in the afternoon and maybe a couple spoonfuls of whatever he was eating in the evening.

"What are you reading?" Her voice was raspy with sleep and she smelled of her usual strawberries. She glanced at the cover as she sat beside him on the sofa, laying her head on his shoulder. "I love that book. It's magical, the whole series. Too bad there's not a magical wardrobe that we could go through to get away from all this." She sighed and got up from the sofa, leaving soft fragrance in her wake. "I'm going to eat."

Sky tossed the book on the sofa and followed her through the dim house to the kitchen. A warm summer rain fell outside, lending some freshness to the air, but without the help of the sun, the interior of the house with its boarded up windows was gloomy and dark. The battery powered lanterns did little to chase away the overall depressed feeling.

Sky watched as she prepared yet another dehydrated meal, using the bottled water and the various packets of food to create an edible meal. He'd been eating well for the past two weeks and it was all because of her. Which made what he wanted to say that much more difficult.

"Jude."

"Yes?"

He couldn't tell her, not right now. "Nothing." He raised his hand and waved it vaguely. "I'm going to take a quick check outside, make sure nothing's doing."

"All right," her voice was so calm and normal, as if she were preparing dinner on any normal summer evening. "This will be ready in about fifteen minutes."

"That's fine." He left, unwilling to upset her moment of calm.

* * * *

Zombies, if you were prepared, were pretty easy to kill. It was the thinking, reasoning humans who wanted to rob, rape and murder that he worried about. They could surround them, set the house on fire, do whatever. He had to get it through to her that there was safety elsewhere and holing up in this house wasn't the answer.

"Jude, I've been thinking. We should…"

Jude's fork stopped halfway to her mouth. Brown reconstituted gravy dripped from the plastic tines, making a soft patter on the paper plate.

"Don't want to hear it, Sky. My house is an oasis, a refuge from the chaos and uncertainty in the streets." She dropped the fork in favor of a paper towel, which she immediately started to shred. "I'm not leaving." Spotting the crank radio on the table, she pushed it away from her.

"A refuge can turn into a prison awful quick," he told her as he took the paper towel from her and wiped his mouth. "Say there's another wave of zombies. Next time we might not be so lucky."

"No zombies have been around the house since the last time," she tapped her fingers on the wooden table, pushed the vase an inch to the left. "You've seen that for yourself. Why leave here? It's safe and we have plenty of supplies." She studied him for a moment, her expression changing from one of defiance to one of anxiety. Her voice was an uncertain whisper. "Did I do something? You don't like me anymore?"

"Jude, sweetheart, that's not it." He patted her hand, squeezed it to reassure her. "You're misunderstanding me—"

She rushed on before he could finish. "It *is* safe, Sky, I've been safe here for over a month before you got here."

"Things'll change. Tell me how safe it's gonna be where there's about fifty of them outside the window. More of them coming until all you can hear is their shuffling and groaning." He saw the fear rising in her eyes, but he forced himself to continue. "Then they start to press against the house, the windows, the doors. How long do you think this old house is going to stand up, Jude? Even the iron gate isn't safe if there's enough of them."

Jude stared at him, hands clenched. "Are you trying to scare me? Because it's working."

"I'm just trying to talk some sense into you."

"Fuck you!" She jumped up from the table. "Nobody's keeping you prisoner here. You can leave any time. "

He followed her, reached out for her. The last thing he wanted her to do was be angry. "Jude, baby, please, no." Sky grabbed her arm and held her tight. "I want you to go with me."

She shook her head, her hair flying around her face like a curly nimbus. "I don't want to go. I don't want to leave here. You know how bad it was out there." Her eyes flashed. "Why would I want to go back out there?"

Sky stroked her arm, tried to make her see reason. "That was because you were alone. You'll be with me. We'll find other people, band together."

"No! That never works. There's always arguing, fighting, crazy people." With a muffled sob, she shook his hand off her arm and sat on the sofa, knocking a book to the floor. "It's better to stay here."

"You're living in your own tomb, Judith." He had never felt so helpless and torn in his life. Couldn't leave her here, couldn't stay. What was he supposed to do?

Tears glistened in her eyes as she stared at him. "At least I know where and how I'm going to die. I have control over that. Out there," she shook her head. "Out there is a crap shoot."

"What about your brother? Didn't you say he was in Alabama? We could go look for him. Maybe there are camps, refugee camps set up." *Why couldn't she see reason?*

"I told you no." Her voice was flat.

He was fighting a battle that he didn't have the weapons to win.

"Jude—"

"No!" She shrieked at him, her hands balled into fists. "Don't ask me--"

A burst of static from the shortwave tore through the tense air between them. It sounded as if someone was twisting the dial, trying to find a clear signal. Jumbles voices, static, garbled music filled the air.

Both of them froze, and then turned in the direction of the radio.

"What—" Sky snapped his mouth shut.

"Shhh!" Jude jumped up from the sofa and grabbed his arm, her fingernails biting into his skin.

A female voice spoke through the tinny speakers. *"If you can hear this broadcast, please listen carefully. If you are now in any Northeastern state from Maine to Delaware, all of New York and Pennsylvania. Refugee camps have been set up in Shady Oaks , North Carolina, Whitehurst, Tennessee and Olla, Louisiana. Get to these camps if you can. If you are in the Northeast, please leave as quickly as you can, if you are able. Try to make it to these camps. Stay away from large cities. More information..."* the broadcast ended in a burst of static.

Unable to find a pencil, Sky had scratched the information into table using the tines of a fork.

"Shady Oaks, North Carolina. Whitehurst, Tennessee. Olla, Louisiana." Jude repeated in hushed awe. "Camps. Government camps? Oy, FEMA."

"Whitehurst is next door to Anderson, where my folks live. This means they might be okay, they might have survived." He turned to Jude, who was still staring at the radio. On her face was an expression torn between hope and disbelief.

"Who knows if it's even accurate?" Jude shrugged her shoulders. "It might be a tape loop, or false information." She didn't meet his eyes, looking instead at the boarded up windows. "It could be anything."

Sky took her hands in his. Though tenuous, the radio broadcast was a wedge he could possibly use to get her moving, get her out of the mindset that she had to stay there. "But it's a chance. We can go, find out what's going on." He squeezed her hands, stroked them, then turned up a palm and kissed the warm surface. "Please, Jude."

She wouldn't look him in the eye.

Her hands trembled in his and he squeezed tighter.

"I don't know, I don't know. I can't just go on the strength of one broadcast."

He closed his eyes, let his breath sigh out through his nose. *What else did she need to convince her?* "What if it doesn't repeat, Judith? You going to stay here anyway?"

"I don't know," she repeated. "I just don't know."

Sky dropped her hands. "I'm going." As soon as the words were out of his mouth, he wanted to take them back.

"Sky, you can't go. You have to stay! You have to!"

"No, Judith." As much as it hurt him, he refused to let his feelings for her get in the way of his freedom. He didn't want to die in that house and he knew she didn't want to either, despite what she said. It was just a matter of convincing her otherwise.

She stared at him and he could see her mind racing, her expression tightening.

"Then go." She waved a hand at him. "Take whatever you need. There's plenty."

"Jude."

"Go." She ran upstairs and slammed their bedroom door.

CHAPTER TWELVE

For the rest of the day, Sky sat in front of the radio, listening for any other broadcast that would wend its way through the static. Jude, emerging from her self-imposed exile, wandered into the dining room at one point, ran her fingers over the words she had scratched into the dining room table. Night fell and Jude joined him in his vigil, sitting on the living room sofa while he sat at the table.

"It's not going to repeat," Sky rubbed his face with his hands. His eyes were tired, red-rimmed. "Are you going to trust me? Because the last thing I want to do is leave you here."

Jude sat on the sofa and stared at him. She could see the dark shadow of his beard along his jaw line and his golden brown hair stood up in ragged spikes on his head. Though she didn't want to admit it, he was right. She couldn't stay here indefinitely. Either the zombies would get her or the looters would. And no amount of guns would stop them even if the both of them stayed. She didn't really believe Sky would leave her here, but he had family in Tennessee. What did she have to offer him here?

Jude got up, crossed the room and laid a hand on his shoulder. It was solid and firm. She'd felt his arms around her; even as he slept she knew she was protected and safe. She didn't want to lose that.

"Sky." Her voice was soft. "Let me think about it, okay? "

He took her hands in both of his. "Please, Jude. I'm not sure if I can leave you here."

* * * *

A few days later, Jude joined him on the back deck. "I thought you were leaving today?"

Sky shrugged. "It's too hot and humid." He took a toke from the joint that burned between his fingers.

"Yesterday it was too cloudy." Jude fluffed out her hair and gazed over the expanse of backyard. The strawberries had given up, the tomatoes were petering out,. and the zucchinis were being stubborn with their yield. Maybe she would have a couple more good weeks and that was it.

"I didn't want to walk in the rain. It could have rained, you know."

"Then grab a car."

He shrugged again. "Maybe."

"Hey," she snapped her fingers in front of his face. "You're not responsible for me. I'm not one of your students that you have to save."

He stared out at the expanse of the backyard, took another toke. "Lucky for you with the concrete wall."

"My dad had that done when he started working for EID." She scrunched down on the patio cushions. "So your family lives on a farm?"

"Not a farm exactly. Patch of land with a house." He turned his head. "What's the EID?"

"Ediburgh Infectious Diseases."

He turned his entire body toward her now, giving her his full attention. "Your father worked with infectious diseases."

Now it was Jude's turn to shrug. "I told you that. Stuff like strep throat, staph, blah blah."

"And he got infected at work, you said?"

"Oh, *that* you remember." She was alarmed at the probing expression on his face. "What exactly are you asking me? Maybe they used the place as a clinic, I don't know."

"But it was a corporation?"

"All I know is by the time I got back here they were dead. Who knows what happened."

He stared at her for a while longer then nodded. "Okay, yeah. Who does know what happened. But you never wondered? Your dad, working for this infectious diseases corporation? What did he do?"

"Research, I guess. Look." She was tired of this line of questioning. "I was in grad school. I didn't concern myself about what he was doing."

"As long as your bills were paid, right?"

Jude narrowed her eyes. *Who the hell did he think he was?* "For someone who is afraid of heights, you sure are up on your high horse. You don't know shit about me or my family."

To her surprise he laughed, a low, knowing laugh that made her shiver despite her anger. "I know a lot more about you than you think."

"That's not the point."

"But I think you don't know a lot about what your dad did either."

"That's neither here nor there."

"'Course not." He closed his eyes and settled back, a smug smile on his face. "Forget I said anything."

She wanted to slap him.

****

After a lunch which she ate standing up in the kitchen to avoid conversation with Sky, she decided to go in the backyard, pay a visit to her parents' resting place. Jude sank down in the damp grass and pulled weeds that had taken shallow root. They weren't here to advise her anymore and what advice they had given her was neither applicable nor useful. *Go to school, Judith, get your degree, Judith, secure a good job.* What good was that now?

Sitting there, she closed her eyes and heard nothing besides the wind whispering through the trees. The sounds of nature, birds chirping, cicadas chattering, squirrels rustling through the trees. There was very little of that now. The world around her was as silent as a cemetery at midnight.

That's how it's going to be when he leaves, Jude. You're living in your own tomb.

Sky's words came back to her as she sat there, grieving over people who weren't there anymore. What was she planning on doing for rest of her life? Read books, look at family photos, stay high until she couldn't bear one more dreary, lonely day?

And there would be no Sky. She could smoke until she couldn't hold her head up and that ache would never diminish. She might as shoot herself as soon as he left because she would be dead anyway.

* * * *

"The chocolate fountain at the buffet. I loved that." She paused. "That buffet was the best. I think they had ex-cons cooking the food."

"Went on a field trip there. Kids were sticking their fingers in the fountain and licking them."

"You went on a field trip to a buffet?" Jude snorted. "Is that what they've been teaching?"

"They had seen a play and went to eat. I just heard they were going to eat and I volunteered to chaperone."

"How many of those high school girls tried to sit next to you on the bus?" Jude elbowed him. She switched to a high falsetto. "I wanna sit next to Mr. Beckett, he's just so cuuuuuuute!!"

"Yeah, you had to be careful with that." He yawned. "You could get in a lot of trouble. Those girls." He shook his head. "Talk about hot pants."

"I bet. Your turn."

They played a game of 'what did you miss from before' and tonight's topic was restaurants. Despite them going their separate ways during the day, they always came together at night, neither of them wanting to be alone in the dark.

"There was a barbeque place."

"It's always barbeque in the south, I swear. Barbeque, beer and..." she searched for another "b" word. "Bullshit"

"That's lame, Jude. You gonna let me finish?"

She exhaled loudly. "Go ahead. Do they serve the food on a garbage can top? I saw that on the Food Channel."

Sky snorted laughter. "No, they gots paper plates n shit. But only on Sundays."

Jude paused. "Are you serious?" She sat up in bed and looked at him in the dim light. He seemed serious, but his eyes were sparkling with contained laughter. "You're so full of it." The mattress squeaked as she flopped back down. "Go on."

"They serve really good barbeque out of the back of a church. Homemade sauce and everything."

"Ol' black momma cooking over a woodstove?" Jude was overcome with giggles. "With a cigarette hanging out of the corner of her mouth and a razor in her shoe?"

"That's so stereotypical. Besides, they weren't cigarettes, they were those little cigarillos. Cheaper, I bet." He nudged her. "At my school, they'd send you to sensitivity training."

"I'm extremely sensitive," Jude said. "Really, I am. What's the name of the place? Does it begin with 'old'?"

Sky paused. "You know, I don't know. All I know it's on some road behind the Baptist church."

"I bet the name of the road begins with 'old'." She continued to tease him.

"If you come with me, you can find out for yourself."

"All right then, I will. I'll go with you."

He sat up and peered at her through the semi-darkness. "You'll go with me," he repeated. "What made you change your mind?"

"I want to eat barbeque off a garbage can lid. Besides, I've never been to Tennessee."

He put his arms around her and kissed her on the lips, a loud smack. "You're the best, Jude."

"You weren't going to leave without me, anyway," she whispered. "Admit it."

He shook his head. "I couldn't."

CHAPTER THIRTEEN

The crash of metal against metal jerked him out of a mid-afternoon nap. Jude's body lay against his, her skin warm and damp. His first instinct was to dismiss it as a dream, roll over and lose himself against her naked skin, but then he heard a revving motor and muffled screams.

People. There were people out there.

"Jude... you hear that?" He turned to her to find her awake, eyes wide and blinking. "Sounds like a car accident." He slid out of bed and began pulling on clothes. "Engine's still running." A car horn broke the silence, sounding over and over again until it was one long blare. "Jesus Christ, they're gonna call every zombie within a five mile radius."

"Oh, for goodness sake." Wild curls stuck against the side of her face and her eyes were puffy with sleep. But she heaved her lovely naked body out of bed and began to dress. "You know they're probably already dead." Blue underwear slid over her hips. Bra, t-shirt and jeans followed. "I'm only going out there to quiet that damn horn."

Sky pulled his t-shirt over his head. "I'll make you a deal. You shut off the car horn, I'll take care of the survivors." Gorgeous woman, but she had a heart of damn stone. "Let me worry about that."

She sucked in her cheeks. "I should have left your boy-scout ass back at the goddamn CVS."

"If you shoulda and coulda, you woulda." Sky laughed at his own joke as he laced his boots.

"Oh, fuck you." He ducked the pillow she tossed at his head.

"Save that for later, baby." He grinned at her exasperated look.

Mumbling to herself, she stomped into her boots, fluffed out her hair with both hands and glared at him.

"Let's go and earn a fucking rescue badge."

* * * *

"Where the fuck did they come from?" Sky yanked at the door of the mid-sized car. The metal shrieked, reluctant to yield and give up its bounty. The driver's bloody head lolled against the headrest while Sky fought to open the door. *Doesn't look so good for him.*

Jude looked away, her palm slick against the pistol's grip as she scanned the street. A fifty-foot walk up the street had her sweating in the harsh afternoon heat. If the crash didn't attract the zombies, the revving motor and the blaring horn would.

She breathed a sigh of relief when the engine and the horn quieted, but kept up her vigil, her gaze scanning the street for any movement.

"What's going on?" She didn't bother to glance behind her. The moans of the passengers told her more than she wanted to know. "Are they alright?"

"No." Sky's voice was sharp, and she risked a quick look over her shoulder. A man and two women. It was a split second before she realized that the man wasn't wearing a red shirt but a white shirt that was soaked with blood. "Help her."

Jesus. She grabbed the arm of the black-haired woman whom Sky had helped out of the back seat of the car. "Come on." Jude flicked her eyes up and down the block. Everything seemed fine, but that was just when things would sneak up on you. "Let's get them inside. No telling if we're going to get any dead visitors." The curtain in the picture window at the Campbells' house shook and then was yanked down. She turned her gaze away.

"No." The driver, a heavy, swarthy man wheezed. Blood ran down his arm, dripped from his wrist. He lowered his voice and spoke directly to Sky. "I'm bit."

Sky's eyes met hers and then away, his face expressionless. "Shit." His eyes were sad, but his hand went to the butt of his gun on his hip.

"Brian, no!" The dark haired, pale woman yanked away from Jude and put her arms around the injured man's neck. "You'll be fine. We have help. These people...."

Brian allowed her to embrace him and then placed his hands around her waist, nudging her away. "No, Louise." His voice was gentle. "I'm hurt too bad. And I'm bit."

A short, tan woman with blonde, curly hair scrambled out of the car and stood blinking in the late afternoon sun.

Brian placed a hand on her shoulder, his breathing heavy." Katie, go with these people." He looked at Sky. "What's your name?"

"Sky Beckett."

"Brian Woods." The two men shook hands and Brian glanced at Jude. "This your wife?"

Sky blinked. "Yeah. Her name's Judith."

"That's Katie Woods, my sister, and her friend, Louise Wells." He indicated each in turn and there were murmured greetings.

Coughs racked Brian's body and he leaned against Sky, catching his breath. "Jude. Jude. Hey, Jude, The Beatles. Jude the Obscure. Thomas Hardy. The criticism was so great, it made him stop writing novels."

Jude closed her eyes for a second and forced her lips into a smile. This guy knew he was a dead man and made small talk anyway. Tears pricked the corners of her eyes and she sniffed. "I like it," she said. "So much better than Judy. I never read Jude the Obscure. I did hear that they burned it, banned it."

The smile on his face matched hers. "Yep." He coughed again. "If it was published these days, no one would bat an eye. It would be nothing."

"These days, there is nothing." She rubbed her left hand over her mouth, still holding the gun loosely in her right.

Brian waved his hand between her and Sky. "You guys got each other, right? That's something." He turned back to Katie, who was standing off to the side. "I'm going to take a walk with Sky here."

Each woman came to him in turn and hugged him. He kissed each of the women's cheeks, each breath an effort. Tears glistened in Louise's bewildered eyes and Katie was sobbing.

Jude caught Sky's eye. *Back of the head,* she mouthed. Her heart was a lump of cold in her chest. The death and killing would never, ever stop.

He jerked his head in a quick nod. "Come on, Brian." He put an arm under the man's shoulders. "Let's walk."

She watched him go for a moment, Sky's tall frame supporting the shorter, wider man. With a sigh, she turned to the women. "Katie, right?" She addressed the blonde woman, who nodded, her face ashen. A heavy wool coat was wrapped around her shoulders.

Louise spoke in a loud voice. "Your husband is going to kill him?"

Jude gave a noncommittal shrug. "I don't know what they're going to do. All I know is that your friend said he was bit. You should know by now what that means."

Louise shook her head, tears rolling down her round cheeks. "I swear, I told you guys. We should have left sooner." She sniffed, lifting the hem of her t-shirt to wipe her nose. Her belly button was pierced.

Jude's temper snapped. *Why couldn't people adapt to the circumstances?* "Let's get inside." She was turning to lead them into the house when a single shot rang out. Shards of ice lanced through her stomach and she looked at the two women frozen in place next to her.

Katie broke down crying, braying open-mouthed sobs that shook her slight body. Louise put her arm around her, smoothed the blonde's hair, murmuring soothing words.

Jude wandered a few feet away, eyes still scanning the landscape. She would let them have their moment of grief, then she would usher them inside. Between the horn, the crash and now the crying, there was too much noise.

She squinted up the street, the setting sun turning everything a warm shade of orange.

Where was Sky?

CHAPTER FOURTEEN

J ude waited longer than she should have with the two women. Despite the brave face she'd put on, she was deathly frightened. What if Sky didn't come back? She pushed the thought away as soon as it popped into her mind, not wanting to dwell on something over which she had no control. Taking a deep breath, she forced herself to be calm even as anxiety brewed in her stomach. It shouldn't take that long. He'll be back in less than fifteen, maybe twenty minutes, right? Right? God, she hoped so. *Please.*

Next to her, the two women huddled together, holding each other even as they perspired in the oppressive heat. The blonde woman with the coat, sobbed as the brunette woman whispered to her, squeezing her shoulders in what looked like a bone-crushing embrace. Holding the pistol in her hand, she turned toward the women and they both jumped.

Jude closed her eyes briefly, fought for composure. With Sky gone, she was in charge now. It was her job to make sure everyone remained calm.

"I'm not going to shoot you." She pushed the corners of her mouth up in what she imagined was the worst smile ever. "I promise, I'm not." Placation had never been her strong suit--she preferred to distance herself from people who were out of control--but in this circumstance she had no choice.

"Yeah, right." Louise's dislike for her showed on her face, the way she frowned when Jude spoke to her. "You don't look too stable to me." She spat on the ground and pulled Katie closer. "You're a fucking time bomb."

Katie pulled at Louise's arm. "Lou, come on, don't do that. "

Jude bit at the inside of her cheek, resisting the urge to slap Louise in her smug, freckled face. Nothing but trash, this one. Too many personalities in one house wasn't going to work. She glanced up the street again, searching for Sky. He should have been back by now.

"Let's go inside," she said, no enthusiasm in her voice. If Sky didn't come back, it would be her and the ladies, so she might as well get used to it. She grimaced with distaste.

Louise and Kate stared at her, not moving. With one last look up the street, Jude turned and marched to her front porch. If they followed, they followed. If not, then, whatever. The scuff of soles on the blacktop indicated that they had managed to swallow whatever suspicion they had of her.

Besides, what other choice did they have?

****

Jude handed Katie a bottle of water and placed the other bottle on the table in front of Louise. They cried and whispered to each other and she moved to the living room, not desiring to intrude on their private moment of grief. But she couldn't sit still. Instead she revisited the porch, staring down the street into the deepening gloom until her eyes watered with the strain. The sun was setting now, spreading orange light through the deserted neighborhood, but still no signs of Sky.

Adrenaline made her jumpy. She wanted to go looking for Sky, to search every backyard on the block until she located him. But she couldn't leave these stupid girls here unattended. *Damnit, Sky.*

When she went back inside for the third time, Katie gave her a mournful look. She was so thin and small, hunched inside the coat that Jude felt a surge of sympathy in her chest that overpowered her own loss.

"I hope your husband is okay." Katie gave her a small smile.

Save it, Jude wanted to say, but she nodded, tears stinging her eyes. Blinking rapidly, she said, "He'll be back any minute now." Her voice shook and she turned away, fighting for control. Louise just stared, offering no words of sympathy.

"Where are you two from?" Might as well as have some conversation. Sitting around in silence never accomplished anything. "Are you hungry? There's plenty of 'add your own water' food around here."

Jude forced a smile, playing the pleasant hostess, anything to keep the gnawing fear that Sky wasn't coming back away from her mind. She strode to the kitchen and began rustling through her bags of trail mix, bringing the bounty of dried food to the table, to her new friends.

"So where are you all from?" She smiled and popped a piece of dried fruit in her mouth, chewed and swallowed it without pleasure or taste.

Katie pulled the overcoat around her, hunched over her water bottle. "We're from Breslin, up in North Jersey."

Her voice was small, soft. A small, nervous hand brushed back a strand of blonde hair. "We were there for a while, hiding out. Then we wanted to make a break for it, get out of there before things got too heavy. "

"Brian wanted to find some survivors." Louise spoke now, her brash voice loud in the silence. Her dark hair was long and stringy, pulled back in a ponytail. "He wanted to join up with other people." She fiddled with the diamond stud in her ear. "Maybe not such a good idea." She sniffed and looked away.

Jude kept smiling and nodding. *If you had stayed put, Sky would be here right now.*

Katie, nodded too and drank more of her water. "He thought we would be able to find some sort of government camp." Her complexion was surprisingly pale.

Louise tapped the table with her bottle. "They've got to be out there somewhere. The government just hasn't collapsed totally. I'm sure they've got the President in a bunker somewhere until they figure out a cure."

"If there even is one. " Jude paced to the crack in the boards again, peeked out. Nothing. Dusk had fallen now, the world outside the window gone to shadows. Something had happened, it must have. He wasn't coming back. She barricaded the door, holding on to the wooden plank for a long moment before turning around and lighting the lanterns.

Her heart slowed until it was moving at a snail's pace, then become so erratic in its rhythm that she had to sit down on the sofa to catch her breath. *He's not coming back.*

Finally, she turned to the two women who looked more frightened than ever. They knew were the blame for her loss. If they had stayed their asses up wherever they came from or at least took a different route, she'd be buzzing right now, lightheaded with weed, tracing the tattoos on Sky's arms, comfortable in their own little cocoon.

None of the women spoke for a long time. Jude tugged at her hair and walked into the kitchen. Like a busy den mother, she began distributing more packs of trail mix, freeze dried meals and desserts. After passing out utensils and more bottles of water, she brought them to the door of the basement.

"You can sleep down there. I'll get water for you to wash up with in the morning. I'm going to sleep. Please, do not come upstairs in the middle of the night or I will shoot you. If you need me, and you have to think very carefully if you really, really need me, yell for me from the bottom of the stairs. Is that clear?"

Louise sucked her teeth and crossed her arms. "Why do we have to sleep in the basement?"

Jude's fingers flew to the butt of the pistol on her hip. "Because it's *my* house. If you don't like it you can sleep outside, or find your own damn house. There's plenty of them on the street." She was snarling and she tried to back off, calm herself down. The nerve of this woman! "Any other questions?"

They both shook their heads, their eyes wide. Was she being foolish, too trusting? These people were literally off the street, refugees whom she took at face value, believed their stories. They could easily kill her in the middle of the night just for kicks.

Damn you, Sky. Infecting me with your do-gooder teacher germs.

Let them, she thought, walking through the living room. Who cares?

Louise spoke. "Thank you for taking us in."

"Yes." Jude climbed the stairs, her feet heavy on each tread. She'd lied to them. She wasn't going to sleep at all.

* * * *

Alone in the bedroom, she sat on the edge of the bed, grabbed a joint from the box and took four heavy hits in quick succession. She wanted her head to be out of this nightmare, at least for a brief period of time. A hot breeze wafted through the windows, bringing with it the almost sweet summer evening smell. Another three hits and she ground out the joint in the ashtray. The drug invaded her mind and she was floating, blissfully detached from reality. A dreamy smile spread across her face as she stripped down, leaving only her panties and tank top. Gun tucked underneath her pillow, flashlight on the nightstand, she lay back on the pillow and drifted into sleep, too stoned to cry.

* * * *

The screams were nothing new, she'd visited them often enough in her nightmares. She rolled onto her side, her hand going to the gun under her pillow in an automatic gesture, knowing the screaming in her head would soon stop. But when they continued, shrieking gasps that tore through the house, she jerked bolt upright in the bed, heart slamming painfully against her ribs.

"Sky?" His name was past her lips before her sleep and pot logged brain realized that he wasn't there. She would have to handle this one on her own.

Jude jumped out of bed, jammed her legs into her jeans and stomped into her boots as the screaming continued.

Lips pressed in a grim line, she snatched her gun from the mattress and galloped downstairs, jumping down the last six treads into the living room.

The basement door was ajar and the screaming had risen in pitch, assaulting her ears with a shrill tense, sound that reverberated through her body. Someone was being murdered down there.

"Not good," she muttered to herself and forced her now shaking legs to take her down the basement steps.

There was a lantern burning in the far corner, leaving much of the basement in shadow, and for that she was grateful. Katie, free of her bundles of clothes, now had Louise by the arm, tearing at the flesh of Louise's hand and wrist. Though Louise screamed and kicked at her, Katie wouldn't let her go.

Jude stared at the mess in front of her, unable to speak. She should have checked Katie for bites. She was so wrapped up in Sky, whether he was coming back or not, that she had neglected the simplest safety precaution.

And she was stupid for trusting them.

"Don't fucking stand there, you stupid bitch!" Louise's face was a mask of horror and pain. "She's killing me!"

You're already dead, Jude thought and walked purposefully over to where the two women were locked in combat. The smell of blood was rich and thick, like a disgusting soup left to fester on the back of a stove, and she swallowed the bile that had gathered in her throat. Her arm reached out of its own volition and nestled the muzzle to the back of Katie's matted blonde hair.

The report of the gun was loud in the confined space and Katie dropped motionless at their feet. Jude bent and pulled the trigger again, blowing most of Katie's brains out onto the cement floor. *Double tap.* She smiled, pleased she had only used two bullets. *Waste not, want not.*

Still smiling, she met Louise's eyes, her hand still vibrating from the two shots. It was in her eyes, she knew it, because Louise took a step back. There was no saving her, she had been bitten. Period.

"We can do this one of two ways, Louise." Jude spoke past the ringing in her ears. "I can bandage you up and put you out." She raised the pistol slightly and Louise retreated another step. "Or I can shoot you right here."

"You're a crazy bitch, you know that?" Louise cradled her injured hand with the other, both pressed against her midsection. Her voice was loud, screechy. "You and your husband. Shooting people. You don't know anything about this disease. Just because we're bit, doesn't mean we'll turn."

Jude's whole body shook and her vision was blurry with tears. She forced a calm note into her voice. "Louise, you know how it is. It can't be helped. Brian knew that. What's your choice?"

The blood dripping from Louise's hand and arm made a pattering sound on the floor.

"Crazy." Louise's voice had lost much of its force. "You'll be alone. Your husband is gone, dead. You'll be alone."

Jude nodded, a tiny smile tugging at the corners of her mouth. Why she was smiling, she had no idea. "I know, Louise. I know. I'll be alone." Back to square one. "Don't force me to make the choice for you."

"You won't shoot me."

Jude sighed. Not the 'you don't have the guts' crap. "Louise. Make your choice or I'll do it for you."

Without another word, Louise bared her teeth and turned away from Jude, running for the stairs. As she ran, her guts spilled out and Jude screamed in horror.

How could she even talk, torn open like that?

Louise tripped over her own intestines, slid in her own blood and fluids until she hit a stack of cardboard boxes labeled "SmartFood Storage" and groaned.

Shaken by the gory scene, Jude swallowed a few times before she was able to aim the gun.

Louise turned over, stared at her, opened her mouth, whether to speak or to scream, Jude didn't wait to find out.

Jude shot her in the face.

Whimpering now, all sense of reality gone, Jude angled the gun and shot her in the back of the head. Three time.

"Stay down," she whispered. "Please, stay down."

Before she turned away, she nudged both bodies with the toe of her boot, satisfied that they wouldn't be getting up again. She grabbed the lantern and took it upstairs, taking one step at a time, her arm tingling from the gun's recoil and her ears ringing with sound of the shots.

Just in case, she barricaded the basement door. She'd take the bodies out in the morning.

In her bedroom, hers and hers alone now, she sat on the edge of the bed and pulled off her boots and jeans.

She crawled into bed and pulled Sky's pillow to her chest. Then and only then did she allow herself to cry.

CHAPTER FIFTEEN

Sleep was the enemy, the darkness in which nightmares that would chase her, grabbing at her with their dead hands. Turning on her side, she hugged Sky's pillow to her nose, breathing in the smell of his sweat and that soap that he favored. Inky blackness surrounded her: she had forgotten to leave one of the lanterns burning. Didn't matter. She was only one moving around up here.

Jude kicked the sheet off her legs and twisted on the bed-clothes, trying to find a comfortable position. The heat was oppressive, even in the middle of the night, humid fingers pressing against her clammy skin. Her heartbeat refused to slow down and she couldn't lie still.

Staring at the dark ceiling, she allowed thoughts to roll through her mind and came to a decision. Tomorrow, at the first glow of dawn, she would look for him. He might be hurt or holed up somewhere. She would go out, find him and everything would be alright. They would leave together after all. Hope lightened her heart and she rolled over, one word echoing through her mind. *Tomorrow.*

Finally immersed in exhausted sleep, she dreamed of a garbage truck that rolled down the middle of her street, grabbing zombies with a mechanical hand and dumping them in the compactor area of the truck. The compactor would then crush them, resulting in a stinking mush of putrefied human tissue. A heavy, meaty smell emanated from the truck, like a blood-soaked bandage that had been tossed aside. The stench clogged her nose, choking her until she awoke, a cough caught in her throat.

She strained her ears in the dark, trying to hear over the whispering silence. Was it her fevered imagination, or did she hear something? The basement door was barricaded, of that she was sure. Were those the sounds of the house creaking or was someone here? The old blood smell was still here. Did the wind change, bringing a wave of dead body stench across town?

A thumping sound, a small soft, *whump*, came from the hallway.

Jude's hand crept toward her gun. She pointed the gun in the direction of the door, her finger curling against the trigger.

She couldn't see a damn thing but she didn't want to take a chance with the flashlight. A small sound came from her throat.

"Jude, it's me."

"Sky?" A yellow ray of joy bloomed in her chest. She dropped the gun and scrabbled for the flashlight, fingers fumbling at the on switch.

He held up his hand, shielding his eyes against the strong, shaking beam of the light.

"Hey, baby. I got us a truck." He spoke as if the words forced themselves from his throat of their own accord, his voice raspy and tired. He turned on the lantern on the dresser next to him.

"I thought you were dead!" She launched herself off the bed toward him, but he held her at arms' length.

Close up, he looked awful and smelled worse. His hair was in matted clumps. One eye was swollen almost shut and he had a scrape along one arm, his t-shirt torn. But the import of what he'd said dawned on her. "You got a truck?"

"Yeah. A truck. But you gotta let me wash up first."

"I don't care." The hours that he had been gone had been too long. She wanted to embrace him, feel him, solid and real, in her arms.

"No." He squeezed her arms tighter, pushed her backwards towards the bed. "Sit down." His voice was tired, but harsh. "Don't touch me. I have to wash up first."

"Okay." When he released her, she sat, her hands clutching each other, desperate to touch him, to feel him. Two tears slipped down her cheeks. "Okay," she whispered. She stared at him in the dim glow as he shed his t-shirt and jeans, the fabric stiff with dried blood and who knows what else. Every movement was slow, deliberate, as if he had to think each motion through. What the hell happened to him? His face told her nothing, the full bottom lip that she loved, missed, compressed into a thin line.

"Give me the flashlight." He left the room with the pile of dirtied clothes and she resisted the urge to follow, to pry, to ask, to probe.

But he had a truck.

****

Wet, clean and still a little soapy, he came back into the room and scooped her into his arms, pushed his face into her hair, kissed her neck. A few dots of foam still stuck in his hair, bundles of frothy scent that were sticky between her fingers.

"Jude." Even as he whispered to her, he was pulling her top over her head and her panties down, pressing his damp face to her stomach and breasts. She embraced him, drew him closer to her, running her hands through his now clean hair. He kissed her neck, bit at the tender skin, his hands tight in her hair. His breath was warm against her, a marked contrast to his cool, damp skin.

His hands roamed across her hot skin, touching her in the places that he knew would affect her the most. Soon, she was wet and writhing underneath him, opening herself to him. His first thrust in her was almost painful and she sucked in her breath, his whispered words of apology in her ear. He grabbed her bottom in both hands, squeezing her flesh until she was sure he would leave finger marks.

"You're warm, you smell so good." His thrusts became faster, more urgent. He buried his face in her hair, inhaling like a drowning man coming up for air. "Jesus, Jude, I missed you."

Jude wrapped her arms around him, her hands slipping across his back. All she wanted in the world was to have him back and here he was, alive and solid and present. She closed her eyes and buried her nose in his shoulder, breathing in the scent of his skin, committing it to memory as he glided into her. She was greedy for him, selfish with the realization that he was the only one she wanted, ever, and goddamn, she was glad he was back.

Her orgasm was fast and hard, blazing over her in a wave of pleasure. She cried out with the force of it, sinking her teeth into his shoulder and digging her nails into his back. Not long after, his body shuddered and he collapsed on top of her with a low moan, his breathing harsh in her ear.

Jude lay there in the dark, eyes closed, one hand absently stroking his arm, her fingers blindly tracing the inked lines along his forearm and biceps. His breathing was deep and even, but she could see by the lantern light his eyes were open.

"Are you going to tell me what happened?"

"Later." He exhaled. "Jude?"

"Yes?"

"I fucking missed you."

"You told me. Before." She swiped the back of her hand across her eyes. "I missed you too. I thought I would die when you didn't come back."

He rolled over, drew her closer to him. "From now on…" He kissed her earlobe. "Where you go, I go. We go together, or not at all."

CHAPTER SIXTEEN

"There are two dead bodies in the basement." Jude passed him the joint and watched the ember illuminate his face as he inhaled. The eye wasn't as bad as she'd first thought, but it looked like he'd been punched. "Katie, the blonde one, had been bitten too."

Sky frowned. "I should've known. The way she was holding the coat around her." He shook his head. "I never should have left you."

Jude stubbed out the joint in the ashtray and slid her body as close to him as possible. If she could crawl inside his skin and stay there, right next to his heart, she would.

"I was more scared for you." She walked her fingers across his belly. "I thought you weren't coming back."

"Almost didn't." He stretched, the scratch on his arm fresh and angry-looking. "I took the guy into the backyard a couple of houses up the street, far enough away. Didn't want y'all to hear the shot."

"We heard it anyway."

He fixed her with his non-injured eye. "You should've been inside by that time, Jude. What the hell were you waiting for?"

"I was waiting for you to come back!"

Sky nodded, pushed out a breath and continued talking to the ceiling. "We're talking, chatting for a couple of minutes. I…" he cleared his throat. "I shot him in the back of the head in the middle of his sentence." He took a shaky breath. "I swear on all that's holy…never again, sweet Jesus."

Jude rubbed his chest with her free hand, the downy hairs tickling the palm of her hand. "Couldn't be helped." Her voice was just as shaky as his. Jude pinched her eyes shut, but even that couldn't stop the memory of Louise's eyes, the blooming of despair in them as she raised the pistol. "You did what you had to do."

"Right after the shot, a shitload of zombies came out of the woods behind the house. Didn't want to lead them in your direction, so I ran the other way." He stopped. "I got lost, surrounded. Ended up diving into a basement. More of them, down there in the dark." He shivered and Jude felt the goose bumps rise on his skin.

"Fucking lucky I'm not dead. Got out of there, hit the jackpot with a flashlight and the truck keys on a hook in their kitchen. Truck was sitting right in the driveway, as nice as you please, with a full tank. " He laughed. "Turned out I was right by that damn CVS. Easy enough to find my way back. And then I had to climb that fucking ladder."

Jude giggled. "You're lucky that I forgot to roll it up."

He kissed her neck, blew on the damp skin. "It's over now." He relaxed against her. "What happened with you, oh great zombie hunter? Bodies in the basement and all."

"No zombie hunter here." Jude shook her head. "Their screaming woke me up. By the time I got downstairs, Katie, the blonde one, had eaten almost half of the other one's arm."

His fingers rubbed her scalp in a soothing motion. "Jude." He sighed. "I'm sorry."

"Louise tried to tell me she was going to be okay. I told her that I would bandage her hand, whatever, but she had to leave. She argued with me. Then tried to run." Jude squeezed his arm, hard. "She tripped on her own guts and I shot her. In the face." She wanted to cry, but only choking sounds came from her throat. Too many tears shed, and now she was all dried up.

"Shhh." He pulled her face to his chest and stroked the back of her neck. The tension drained from her and once again she was safe, protected. "Like you told me, couldn't be helped. Get some rest, okay?"

****

"It's red. Flashy." Jude ran her hand along the side of the truck.

Sky grinned at the incredulous look on her face. He had pulled the truck into the protected circle of the gate at the end of her driveway, but he still glanced over his shoulder as they loaded the truck. If the zombies had come out of the woods just a few houses away, no telling where they were now.

"It's a diesel V-8 engine with an extended cab and eight foot truck bed." He heaved a box of dehydrated food in the cab of the truck. "Citizen's Band radio, GPS...if the satellites are up, we'll be able to navigate anywhere."

Jude's eyes were pleased. "If it's diesel, we can run it on soybean oil from grocery stores along the way. I saw that on the Science Channel."

"No need for gas stations."

Jude propped ten marijuana plants in the back, tucking them carefully between the boxes. She had already packed her jars of the stuff.

Sky eyed her careful ministrations with amusement. "You plan on being wrecked until they fix everything?"

Jude laughed. "I doubt they ever will. But it's useful for commerce, right? I mean..." She tilted her head slightly to the side, thinking. "Money's worthless, so we need tangible goods. Stuff people want."

"Nothing more tangible than a few hits of pot." He tossed another box of food in the cab. Satisfied with the load, he stepped back. "Anything else?"

Jude shook her head. "Extra clothes, water, filters..." she rattled off the list of supplies, consulting the slip of paper she held in her hand.

If there was anything that he could say about Jude was that she was efficient. He shifted a few boxes into place, mindful of her greenery. Efficient, resourceful and despite what she probably thought, pretty self-sufficient.

He leaned his head back and surveyed the clear blue sky. Even the stink of the dead was diminished today, an omen that boded well for their trip. Hopefully, there were enough roads clear for them to make their way out of town and south.

"What are you grinning about?" She was standing next to him them, peering at him with those soulful brown eyes.

Sky slipped and arm around her shoulders and gave her a long, slow kiss. "It's a great day, isn't it? You...me...we're taking a road trip, baby!"

She squeezed his waist, a small smile playing about her lips. "I guess we are. But I need to do one last thing first. I want you to come with."

****

Jude squeezed Sky's hand as she stood by the bare strip of ground that covered her parents' bodies.

The plant that she had placed there was thriving.

She released his hand and knelt in the dry grass, pulling the tiny weeds. It would be the last time she would be able to do so. Kneeling there, she closed her eyes and heard nothing besides the wind whispering through the trees. She thought she heard a few birds chirp, and the distinctive buzz of cicadas echoed through the air.

Goodbye. Goodbye and I love you.

"Judy." Sky's soft voice interrupted her reverie. "We really should get going. I'm sorry."

She rose without rancor and brushed the dirt off her pants. "I know." She took his hand again, the reality of him, of his presence seeping through her, galvanizing her.

They followed the narrow path back to the house in silence and stood next to the truck.

Jude pressed the key into his hand and climbed into the passenger seat. "For the gate. I don't want it back."

She watched as he ambled to the wrought iron gate, unlocked it and left the key in the lock.

She snapped her seatbelt into place and settled in for the ride.

In the driver's seat, Sky turned the key. The engine caught and boomed with a reassuring roar that settled into a contented purr. He grinned and Jude couldn't resist his enthusiasm.

"You ready?"

Jude nodded. "Let's go."

About the Author

D ahlia DeWinters a romance writer who flirts with the dark side. While many of her stories still dabble in the hearts and roses genre, it is often against a sinister backdrop. She is a lover of all things scary, even though she tends either to watch them while gripping her husband's arm or between her fingers. Her enthusiasm for found footage horror, surprisingly, has rewarded her with a few gems. Drawing, fiber arts, and gardening are a few of the things she does in her spare time, when not dreaming up stories of zombies, mysterious happenings in gothic mansions or screening horror films.

Subscribe to the newsletter for updates, horror movie reviews, and other tomfoolery! Find more information here: https://dahliadewinters.com/lobby/

Also by Dahlia DeWinters

Loving Among the Dead

Claimed by the Desert King

Her Dakota Summer

True Blue

La Belle Bete

Also by Zame Hill

Leaves

Duty to the Dead

Anthologies

Forever Vacancy

Deadly Bargain

Herstory: Fiction Honoring Women's History Month